CAPTURED DEBTS
A DEBTS TO RECOVER COLLECTION

MEYARI MCFARLAND

CONTENTS

Author's Note: Jam Crisis	1
Jam Crisis	2
Author's Note: Controlled Edge	17
09:27 am, Wednesday	18
12:27 pm, Thursday	24
11:58 am, Wednesday	31
17:57 pm, Thursday	37
12:18 pm, Wednesday	43
15:03 pm, Thursday	48
18:51 pm, Wednesday	54
Author's Note: Silken Embrace	62
1. Mission Protocol	63
2. Selection	70
3. Dress Up	77
4. Play Time	83
5. Story Time	89
6. Stockings	96
7. Reward	102
Author's Note: Three Sisters	109
1. Denim	110
2. Wax	119
3. Blood	128
Author's Note: Feast of the Senses	137
1. Sound	138
2. Sight	141
3. Taste	143
4. Touch	145
5. Scent	147
Other Books by Meyari McFarland:	151
Author's Note: The Nature of Beasts	152
1. Returning Home	153
Afterword	165
Author Bio	166

Published by Mary Raichle on Smashwords

Copyright ©2013 by Mary Raichle

All rights reserved. No part of this publication may be reproduced or transmitted in any form or by any means, electronic or mechanical, including photocopy, recording or any information storage and retrieval system, without permission in writing from the publisher.

Requests for permission to make copies of any part of the work should be emailed to me_ya_ri@yahoo.com

This book is also available in ebook format from all major retailers.

❦ Created with Vellum

This collection is dedicated to Te for her incredible stories. I love how you present kinky people in love, Te. Thank you so much for everything you do!

OTHER BOOKS BY MEYARI
MCFARLAND:

A New Path
Following the Trail
Crafting Home
Finding a Way
Go Between
Like Arrows of Fate

Out of Disaster

The Shores of Twilight Bay

Coming Together
Following the Beacon
The Solace of Her Clan

You can find these and many other books at www. MDR_Publishing.com. Sign up for our newsletter there and get updates on the latest releases plus a free book!

AUTHOR'S NOTE: JAM CRISIS

Jam Crisis is a bit more personal than most of my stories. When I was younger I had a friend who was severely bipolar. I didn't realize what was wrong until well after we stopped being friends in college. The experience informs a lot in this story though of course my interactions with my friend weren't anywhere near as fraught as Dustin's.

JAM CRISIS

The rustle of the newspaper being pulled open, folded back and then folded again made a shiver of apprehension skitter up Dustin's spine. His heart beat harder, anticipating a shout, an angry comment on the next news article, Master Augustin's coffee mug flying across the room to crash into the far wall. Dustin bit down on his lip, the pain helping control his rapid breathing.

Breathing too fast and too hard might draw attention. Dustin didn't want attention. Attention was bad. Breathing slowly and evenly was good. Being calm was good. The most important thing he had to do was be calm, quiet and unobserved. It was just so hard to stay calm during Master Augustin's unfailing morning ritual of coffee (two sugars, no cream), newspaper and toast with jam.

He'd been Master Augustin's slave for almost two months now. Even with all that time Dustin had no idea what to make of the man. Certainly, physically Master Augustin was exactly what a Master was supposed to be. He was tall, powerfully built with a carefully maintained physique. His graying hair was kept so closely cropped that Dustin wasn't sure if it had originally been sandy blond or ginger red. Every suit that Dustin had seen Master Augustin wear had been perfectly tailored down to exquisite hand top stitching and a little pleat in the back that let him move more freely.

But he didn't act like the Masters Dustin had known and it confused Dustin terribly. There were no beatings that he didn't deserve and couldn't easily bear. Dustin had his own bed, granted a small slave bed with a thin pad and minimal blankets, but it was his and his alone. Master Augustin made sure that Dustin had so much food that he was gaining weight for the first time since he went into the debt slavery program to save his parents from their debts six years ago, not that he'd been very stocky before that.

Most worryingly, his responsibilities were so clearly defined that Dustin didn't need to fear being trapped in mistakes that would lead to punishments.

It confused Dustin. Where were the shouts? The sudden blows? Master Augustin never laughed until he cried. He didn't sing when he was happy. There hadn't been one black mood yet, which was utterly bizarre. His master never even raised his voice to Dustin or anyone else.

He was so calm and reasonable that Dustin lived in dread of the inevitable explosion. If it had been building this long then it would be absolutely horrific when it finally happened. Dustin wasn't sure that he would survive whatever Master Augustin did when his temper finally broke. He'd barely survived some of Master Reyes' punishments when he exploded.

Dustin bit his lip again as his heart rate skyrocketed and his breathing increased to the point that he was panting with his fingernails digging into his naked thighs. Calm, he had to be calm. Never ever draw attention to yourself. Breathe slowly and easily. The Masters don't like slaves who are uppity or troublesome.

The memory of his training master's stern voice as he lectured Dustin on proper behavior for a true slave helped calm his raveled nerves. Yes, he could breathe. That was something he knew that he could do right. Training Master had been proud of Dustin's ability to be still and quiet on command. He would breathe and wait and not worry about what might happen, what should have already happened.

"Dustin," Mater Augustin said as he studied a particular article in the paper. He didn't look in Dustin's direction at all. "Go get me some tea and some of that new bread will you? Not toasted, just a little of jam on it."

"Yes, Master," Dustin said.

He bowed properly even though Master Augustin didn't look at him. His Training Master had always said that it was important for true slaves to be very polite. Once he'd finished the bow, head pressed against the floor for the count of three, both hands on the ground with the fingers spread wide despite how much that hurt his fingers on his left hand, Dustin stood and hurried from the room.

"What to do?" Dustin whispered once the kitchen door was safely shut.

None of the household servants and other employees would show up for another hour so the kitchen was a safe place at the moment. The white marble floor gleamed at Dustin, cold even through the soft slippers his Master had given him the first day here. More marble, green instead of white, gleamed on the counters. Tiny glass tiles glimmered in the backsplash as Dustin gathered what he needed.

Tea was easy. He'd put the kettle on before he'd woken Master Augustin up and it was bubbling nicely. The bread was easy too, as there was only one loaf in the house at the moment, a thick, dark molasses bread that Dustin thought of as peasant food but Master Augustin claimed was gourmet.

Miss Annie would be going grocery shopping today.

She'd said that there was just enough for Master Augustin's breakfast so there was no reason to worry but she was wrong. There was reason, a very good reason. A reason so strong that Dustin's heart started pounding again and his hand shook as he opened the cabinet door to reveal the jam.

"Jam..." Dustin whined as quietly as he could.

It was the jam that made Dustin start shaking in his slippers. How was he supposed to know which variety Master Augustin wanted? There were four varieties in tiny jars that had been arrived with the last load of groceries. All of them were gourmet varieties that had come from the same place as the bread. There was also one big jar that had been made by Master Augustin's niece.

She used the same recipe as Master Augustin's grandmother and he loved it. Every time he had that jam he smiled and was in a good mood but he'd said last night that he was looking forward to something different with breakfast and that had to mean the jam. What else could it mean? Master Augustin never varied his morning routine.

"Which one?" Dustin whispered.

The shaking got worse as he stared at the little row of jam jars. Dustin spread his hands on the green marble countertop, bracing himself so that his knees wouldn't give way. His heart beat so hard that Dustin couldn't hear anything over it. Every panting breath made his throat go drier, to the point that Dustin wasn't sure that he would ever be able to swallow again.

He could smell the tea, fruity and thick, but Dustin's eyes wouldn't move off the line of jam jars. They seemed to mock him, taunting him with promises of beatings. Master Reyes' vicious punishments surged up in Dustin's mind mixing with the lingering pain in his hand and the smell of bread. Dustin's sight narrowed until he couldn't see anything but the biggest jar of jam. It's handwritten label swam in and out of focus in time with the terror-filled memories of Master Reyes screaming obscenities at him as he raped Dustin.

"Dustin?"

The outside noise cut Dustin's legs out from under him. He fell straight down, hands grabbing him so that his head didn't smash against the green marble counter, his knees didn't crack against the white marble floor. It didn't matter that Master Augustin's voice was quiet and gentle, that his hands helped Dustin find the proper position with his ass in the air and his forehead pressed against the floor. He tried to fight the memories back, tried to listen as Master Dustin talked to him, but the quiet tone of Master Augustin's voice changed inside his head into Master Reyes' screams of fury.

"You stupid little piece of trash!" Master Reyes screamed. *"How can you not know what to do? I told you and I told you and you never ever get it right!"*

Dustin sobbed, blood in his mouth as he jerked against the blows that he expected to fall. They didn't. Nothing happened. Another surge of terror washed through Dustin, ripping a desperate whine out of him when he should be quiet and still. Even the memories of his Training Master's beatings when Dustin failed to be quiet didn't stop the whimpers and sobs.

This had to be the point at which Master Augustin finally broke. This would be the explosion. He'd been given such a simple task and he'd failed utterly. The tea had to be cold by now and Dustin hadn't even managed to get jam onto the bread. He was doomed.

Master Augustin's hand rested on Dustin's back.

It was warm, larger than Dustin's narrow hands. Instead of grabbing and twisting, forcing Dustin to move, Master Augustin's hand simply rested there as if to comfort him. But that couldn't be right, it couldn't. Dustin stopped breathing as he tried to figure out what would happen next. Maybe it was the other hand that would strike him or feet. Dustin couldn't even remember the first time he'd been kicked, just that his father had been angry and his mother had been screaming something.

After a moment Master Augustin started stroking his back in gentle, feathery motions that skimmed over the bones along his spine and drifted down the filling gullies between his ribs. It was surprisingly soothing, so much so that Dustin allowed himself to start breathing again. Not that he would have been able to hold his breath much longer. Passing out was much worse than breathing too hard. The worst things happened when Dustin passed out.

Eventually, after long enough that Dustin's hands and legs warmed the cold stone underneath him, Master Augustin very gently hooked his fingers under Dustin's chin to coax him into sitting up. To Dustin's surprise, Master Augustin was sitting cross legged on the floor next to him as if he was an ordinary person instead of a rich and powerful Master.

Dustin automatically cringed, worrying about dust from the floor getting on Master Augustin's perfect suit. A Master shouldn't do such things. He shouldn't act like a slave was important. That's all Dustin was, a slave, a true slave, not even a debt slave who had the potential to earn his way back to freedom and personhood.

"Hmm, you bit through your lip again," Master Augustin said, pulling out a handkerchief to wipe the blood away.

"Sorry, Master," Dustin said, swallowing hard as the panic tried to well up again at having marred himself without permission.

"It's all right," Master Augustin said as his lips curled in a sad little smile. "I can't figure out what set you off though. Did your former master abuse you with jam or something?"

The sheer thought forced a little squeak of laughter through Dustin's aching lips though he did his best to smother the urge to laugh. Slaves didn't get to be amused. He knew that. His Training Master had told him so many, many times, as had Master Reyes. Suppressing his amusement left Dustin even shakier than he had been from the panic attack.

Master Augustin's lips changed from a quick grin into a slowly drooping frown that made his mouth sad and pinched. Long deep lines formed around it. The change made Dustin's heart rate pick up again. His Master was worried and sad and Dustin had made him feel that way.

He didn't dare look at Master Augustin's eyes. Yes, he had permission to do so but he knew better than to actually do it. Eyes were dangerous. Every Master's eyes lied. All slave's eyes revealed far too much, Dustin very much included. Mouths and hands told the truth, not in the words they said but in the postures, the movements themselves. There was truth in motion, not in speech.

Dustin gulped as he realized that he'd been still for too long. He hadn't answered Master Augustin's question. The ever-present anxiety made Dustin's mouth go dry as his hands began to shake. Master Augustin reached over and put his hand on top of Dustin's wrist, anchoring him as thoroughly as if he'd been nailed to the spot.

"Tell me what made you lock up, Dustin," Master Augustin ordered.

"I didn't know which jam to use on the bread, Master," Dustin said, wincing and biting his lip despite the pain when his teeth closed on it.

"No biting," Master Augustin said, tapping one finger against Dustin's lip to make him let go. "Dustin, I have told you this before. If I don't specify, that means that anything is fine. I was looking forward to seeing which one you thought I would like."

His lips went pinched with frustration as he sighed, a sharp, stiff gust of air that felt like the precursor to being beaten bloody. Dustin wanted to press his head against the floor but with Master Augustin's hand on his wrist he didn't dare. It felt so much safer when he was kneeling properly, even though it left his genitals exposed to kicks and abuse.

"That's not—!" Dustin protested before snapping his mouth shut.

"Not what?" Master Augustin asked. "Tell me."

Dustin swallowed hard as the shakes took over his body again. He'd been so careful this whole time not to have any opinions. Opinions were bad. He was a slave. He didn't get to have opinions, not even ones that agreed with his Master.

Opinions changed so rapidly that there was no point in agreeing or disagreeing with anything. It was going to change in a second or a minute or at most a couple of days. Master Augustin rested a large warm hand against Dustin's cheek, anchoring him against the fear except that now the fear was that the grip could be used to haul Dustin close, to grab his hair or ear and make terrible things happen. So many terrible things happened when a Master touched him that way.

The fear of past pain and the inevitability of future agony made Dustin shut his eyes. It didn't keep the tears from betraying him. They welled up and spilled over, creeping down his cheeks despite all his efforts to push the fear and pain away. Masters hated it when slaves cried. They weren't supposed to have any emotions other than joy at serving and willingness to do whatever their Master wanted.

"Oh, Dustin," Master Augustin sighed as he gently, so gently, brushed the tears away. "I'm not upset. I'm only trying to understand what set off the panic attack so that we can avoid it in the future. Please tell me."

"I'm sorry Master," Dustin whispered as more tears fell from his closed eyes. He sniffled and opened them, immediately training his eyes on Master Augustin's mouth. "I was having a hard time choosing because I didn't know which jam would get me punished. I didn't want to choose wrong."

"Punished?" Master Augustin asked, his mouth dropping open in shock. "Dustin, I would never punish you for choosing a jam I didn't like. At most I'd say to throw it away. I wouldn't punish you for breaking a jam jar or any of the dishes or anything like that. I'll only punish you for being disobedient."

The sheer ridiculousness of that statement made Dustin gasp. He was too tired, too frightened, still shaking too hard for this conversation. Dustin whined, his nails digging into his thighs until Master Augustin caught his hands and held them tightly. It didn't make sense. Punishment wasn't something that came from Dustin's actions. It was something that happened whenever the Masters around him thought he needed it, whether Dustin understood the reasoning or not.

"No," Dustin whimpered.

"Yes," Master Augustin said. "Only when you're disobedient. This isn't disobedient, Dustin. You're too frightened to think straight right now. I won't punish you for being afraid or confused or for not knowing something. It will only happen when you deliberately break the rules."

"That's not how it works," Dustin protested, shaking harder as he dared to disagree for the first time in years. The words started spilling out despite everything inside of him that screamed to shut up and nod no matter how much he disagreed. "It's not. It never has been, not with Master Reyes, or my Training Master. It didn't work that way when I was a debt slave or with my parents. That's not right! I don't understand. You never get angry. You never punish me because you feel good or bad or just because I'm there. You're too *calm!* It's…terrifying!"

Master Augustin's mouth grew more and more astonished as Dustin spoke. The sheer astonishment in Master

Augustin's words made Dustin's horrible behavior worse, prompting him to cry and shake and raise his voice as if he was a free person instead of a thing that Master Augustin owned. It was so very wrong but Dustin couldn't make himself shut up not with this impossibility on top of everything else.

He finally found the ability to stop talking when Master Augustin's mouth snapped shut. Dustin found himself pulled to his feet, Master Augustin's hands firm and controlling on his arms. They hustled out of the kitchen and into the sitting room with its comfortable furniture, warm carpets and cream colors.

Dustin always sat on the floor as was proper for a true slave. Master Augustin had given him a very nice floor pillow that was warm and fuzzy and very comfortable but this time Master Augustin pulled Dustin into his lap. He held Dustin close as the shaking and fear turned into confused tears and then the tears turned into exhausted hiccups and coughs at how sore his throat was.

By then Dustin was so exhausted that he could barely move. It really wasn't proper for him to sit in Master Augustin's lap this way but Dustin didn't dare struggle free, not when Master Augustin had such a firm grip on him.

"Dustin," Master Augustin breathed into his hair once he'd calmed, "your former master was insane."

His lips ruffled Dustin's hair, the pressure gentle and comforting despite the shock that turned Dustin's blood to ice water. Dustin froze. He was so tired that he didn't shake but the shock of what Master Augustin had said made it impossible to respond. Insane? How could Master Reyes be insane? His behavior was a little more extreme than other people in Dustin's life but not that much more.

Master Augustin sighed again, his breath gusting over the top of Dustin's head. It was warm and oddly comforting, so much less threatening that the shouts and wild laughter that Dustin was used to. At the same time, Master Augustin kept rubbing Dustin's back in gentle circles instead of pushing him off his lap or forcing Dustin to kiss him or any of the other things that Dustin expected out of a Master.

"I bought you at a vastly reduced price because you were presumed to have been 'spoiled' by having had a Master who was committed for insanity," Master Augustin continued as if Dustin's heart hadn't stopped. "I checked your file once you were mine. Your mother was bipolar, which is a borderline form of insanity that can be managed with the proper medication."

Dustin shivered at the mention of his mother. She'd always been unpredictable but he hadn't thought it was anything special. Now that Master Augustin mentioned it, though, Dustin did remember her taking medicine at times over the years. He was the middle child of five. His oldest brother Andrew had gone into the debt slavery system at eighteen and suddenly they'd had money.

Unfortunately that was when his father had started drinking. The money had gone away quickly but Father had kept drinking and Mother's medicine ran out and wasn't replaced. His second brother Davis had gone into the debt slavery system as soon as he turned eighteen, too. Most of Dustin's friends had older siblings, aunts and uncles who did so he hadn't thought anything of it. The debt slavery system had seemed like the only chance for a better life to him at that point, though it had turned out to be something else entirely for Dustin.

"As far as I can tell," Master Augustin continued in a slow sad voice, "you and your siblings were sold to pay for the medication that would restore her sanity. Your father was a drunkard, and he drank most of the money away. The first Master you were sold to as a debt slave was a bad one who ran up your debt with unreasonable bills, pushing you into the true slavery system."

Dustin frowned, his fingers playing with the buttons on the front of Master Augustin's shirt. He'd thought that was normal, too. Sure, his DDS agent had told him in the beginning that he'd be able to pay down the debt in a reasonable amount of time but it had never happened. He hadn't met a single debt slave who was able to pay off their debt.

"Your entire life you've been surrounded by people who weren't in their right minds for one reason or another," Master Augustin said. He kissed the top of Dustin's head gently. "I think this must be the first time that you've been around someone who is fully in control of himself."

"Nobody... said," Dustin whispered, the fear starting to melt a little bit. He looked up just enough to see Master Augustin's mouth. It looked sad, not angry or ready to punish. "Not when my parents sold me. Not when Master Reyes' men sold me. My Training Master when I was sold as a true slave was worse but that was his job. Master Reyes was really insane?"

"I'm afraid so," Master Augustin said, kissing Dustin's forehead before pulling him back into the cuddle. "There's a lot more that happened that you obviously don't know. I thought you had been told. I should have asked you long ago. It didn't occur to me that you didn't realize that he was insane. He is getting better with treatment from the last report I got. It will be a long, long time before he's out of the asylum and healthy enough to be responsible for a slave though."

Dustin shivered, wondering what an asylum was like and what would be happening to Master Reyes there. He didn't think they'd use beatings and cages and things on a Master but what did he know? He made himself relax against Master

Augustin's shoulder, still wary but too tired to do anything but relax right now.

"No mood swings?" Dustin whispered a little later when nothing had happened besides a hugely comforting back rub. "No beatings for nothing?"

"No, nothing like that," Master Augustin said, his voice an amused deep rumble through his chest. "You've seen me in every mood I've got, Dustin. This is who I am and how I'll always be. Were you afraid when I got mad last week?"

"Yes," Dustin nodded, swallowing hard. He'd been terrified actually.

"What happened when I got angry?" Master Augustin asked, his hand rubbing Dustin's back again.

"You threw a cup at the wall and then apologized for making a mess," Dustin said, still puzzled by the apology. "Then you cleaned it up yourself instead of having me do it."

"That's the worst that's going to happen if I get angry," Master Augustin said, so firmly that Dustin was tempted to believe it was true, at least right now. "If I'm angry at you, I'll throw something at the wall, watch it break, send you off to your bed to wait and then calm down before I punish you. I'm never going to punish you while I'm angry and I'll certainly never punish you when I feel good. What you've seen so far is exactly what will happen in the future. Do you think you can get used to that in time?"

Dustin opened his mouth to automatically say yes but nothing came out. He didn't know. He honestly didn't know if he could deal with it. The fear of random punishments went so very deep that he didn't know if he could handle it. He didn't know if he could stop watching for them, calm down and be what Master Augustin wanted, not that he really knew what Master Augustin wanted from him.

"I don't know," Dustin whispered, tiny little trembles

shaking his arms and legs. He was too tired for the real shakes. "I don't know if I can stop watching for it, Master."

"You're an excellent slave, Dustin," Master Augustin said, kissing his forehead again. "What you've been doing is fine. I hope that you'll get over the fear in time so that you won't lock up like you did in the kitchen, but it's okay if you keep doing it. I'll be careful not to give you choices that might overwhelm you in the future. We'll keep working on it."

Dustin nodded as he thought that over. A yawn escaped his mouth when he wasn't paying attention to physical things. Master Augustin chuckled and shifted Dustin off of his lap. He laid Dustin down and covered him up with a blanket, patting Dustin's head gently even though it was horribly inappropriate for Dustin to sit on the furniture, especially under Master Augustin's favorite red blanket.

"Rest, Dustin," Master Augustin ordered. "I don't want you to do any of your duties when you're this exhausted. I'll take care of breakfast myself."

Dustin smiled, hiding it in the upper edge of the blanket. He wanted to look up at Master Augustin's face but that was too daring, too incorrect. Instead he watched the calm solidity of Master Augustin's legs. There were no twitches, no bouncing, nothing but calm stability as he straightened up and headed for the door to the kitchen.

"Master?" Dustin dared to call, watching his Master's hands and legs for any signs that he'd done something wrong.

"Yes?"

Master Augustin turned back, his hands relaxed and loose as if nothing inappropriate had happened. He didn't seem to be upset in the slightest that Dustin had interrupted his movement, called attention to himself. If anything, the way he turned to fully face Dustin implied that he was glad that

Dustin had spoken up, that he wanted to hear what Dustin had to say.

"Thank you," Dustin said. He smiled into the blanket again and then yawned hugely.

"For what?" Master Augustin's voice sounded amused as he shifted his weight onto one leg as if he'd cocked his head and smiled at Dustin. He didn't look up at Master Augustin's face to confirm it.

"For…"

Dustin tried to figure out what to say. How could he explain that it was for being kind, gentle, patient, *sane* in an insane world? That Master Augustin deserved so many thanks for not beating him, starving him, raping him, or even being cruel. He truly deserved all the thanks that Dustin could give for every little kindness that he'd gotten in the last two months, as well as for every cruelty that hadn't materialized. And for not considering Dustin 'spoiled' because of what he'd been through in life.

"Everything, Master. Thank you for everything."

"You're welcome, Dustin," Master Augustin said, his voice deep and happy. "Sleep. I'll wake you up when I need you. If you wake up before then, come find me and I'll assign duties to you."

"Yes, Master," Dustin whispered, already falling asleep as the promise of future kindness and the exhaustion from his fear sucked him under.

THE END

AUTHOR'S NOTE: CONTROLLED EDGE

I'm honestly not sure where this one came from. In general, I'm terribly uncomfortable getting into the minds of truly murderous people. Writing from Berta's point of view was difficult in many ways. She's very much a part of her world, valued explicitly for being so dangerous. But that doesn't make it easy to handle being in her mind.

09:27 AM, WEDNESDAY

APRIL 28, 2012

Berta strode through the elegantly wood paneled walls of Master Boles' private home, scanning everyone around her for weapons, inappropriate behavior or other signs of threat. This was only the third time that she'd been called to a private meeting with master Boles. Whatever was going on had to be a major threat to the household. The previous two times had resulted in over a hundred dead on the other side and dozens wounded among the staff.

Of course, calling the estate a 'private home' was something of a misnomer given that Master Boles employed over five hundred people at this location alone and ran the estate like a military compound. The defenses alone took a third of the staff count but it was necessary given his private war with the terrorist Black.

"Maybe we have a lead on Black's location," Berta thought, her steps picking up speed from sheer anticipation.

Killing Black was very high on her list of things to do in life, preferably before Master Boles got involved in the battle. No matter how personal the battle with Black was for Master Boles, it was her job to ensure that he didn't personally fight it out with Black. She and her superior officers frequently discussed how to keep Master Boles out of the impending battle. None of them had come up with anything they thought would be effective but that didn't mean they couldn't keep trying.

"Berta," Jeff Cooper, Master Boles personal assistant and secretary, said as she came in. He bit his lip for a moment before standing and gesturing for her to follow him back into Master Boles' office. "Right this way. He's been waiting for you."

"Trouble?" Berta asked.

"...I'll let him explain it," Jeff replied without meeting her eyes.

Berta frowned. Normally Jeff was eager to discuss any issues that the organization might be having. He regarded information sharing between departments with what Berta thought was a nearly holy fervor, only withholding information when it was specifically security related. She had chastised him several times about it but Jeff had only laughed.

Master Boles' office was several degrees cooler than the outer office, cool enough that goose bumps immediately erupted on the back of Jeff's neck. As Jeff went around Master Boles' massive oak desk to whisper in his ear, Berta stood at attention precisely two inches outside of strike range in front of the desk. Master Boles nodded absently, patting Jeff's arm before gesturing for him to leave. As Jeff left he gave Berta a profoundly sympathetic look, as if his heart hurt for her.

Berta waited until the door shut. "My parents died?"

"No," Master Boles laughed, startled enough that she got several chuckles instead of the more usual smile. "I'm afraid it's rather more urgent than that. I know your plans for when your parents die."

"You are still invited to the wake, Master Boles," Berta

said. "The scotch appears to be aging quite nicely. My friend has come up with some truly lovely fireworks as well."

Master Boles nodded but the smile that her celebration plans usually elicited didn't manifest. Instead he sighed and pushed a thick manila folder across the desk to her. Berta waited until he nodded approval for her to approach before taking the folder. Seeing her lover Adalina's name on the tab made Berta frown far more intensely than she normally allowed herself in Master Boles' presence.

"What did she do?" Berta asked as she flipped open the folder.

Logs showing attempts to access restricted files from Berta's computer system at times when she absolutely had not been present answered the question without Master Boles saying a word. Jeff had been as efficient as always in ferreting out who had attempted to hack the system. Berta growled at realizing that Adalina had been quite thorough in her attempts to circumvent the net nanny controls.

"I am somewhat curious as to why she failed on your computer," Master Boles commented as Berta scanned the records showing that Adalina had succeeded on a dozen other terminals throughout the household. "She's very talented at computer hacking. If she doesn't end up dead from the questioning, I am thinking of putting her into the computer resources department."

"You told me that I was not to work while off the clock," Berta said, snapping the folder shut. She'd seen more than enough already. "I installed one of the best net nannies available on my computer to prevent myself from doing so. There are thirty-seven levels of passwords to get access to anything other than entertainment systems and all computer access is limited to a half hour block before the pop-up reminders begin."

That prompted the laughter that Berta always attempted

to elicit from Master Boles. It was a deep, rolling laugh that filled the room, coupled with a smile that wrinkled his eyes and creased his cheeks. Laughter always transformed him from an intimidatingly severe man into the sort of person that Berta would quite literally follow into hell.

The first time she'd seen that laughter had been during her briefing on arrival as one of Master Boles' debt slaves. Three attempts to murder her previous master had made her 'very unreliable and too dangerous to keep', prompting her resale. The fact that the bastard had tried to rape her repeatedly was apparently not relevant to the Department of Debt Slave Services. Master Boles had been the only one who had bid on her debt, the only one who had seen anything worthwhile in her.

Hearing that rape or attempts to coerce sex would result the aggressor being summarily sold as a true slave had reassured Berta somewhat; seeing Master Boles laugh and smile at Jeff tenderly enough that she hadn't had to be told that they were lovers had convinced her that this man was nothing like the other Masters she had encountered in life.

The possessiveness was expected from a man like Master Boles. What had convinced Berta of his worth had been the tenderness and protectiveness with which he regarded Jeff. Most Masters were convinced that they had rights to their debt slaves bodies. No other that Berta had seen looked at their debt slave lovers with that much blatant love.

It was unique, remarkable, and Berta had dedicated her life to protecting Master Boles and everything he cared for.

"I will deal with her," Berta announced as she set the file on Master Boles desk again.

"Hopefully not like the last one," Master Boles sighed. He leaned his chin on his fist, studying Berta. "I'm still paying for therapy for three of the first responders, Berta."

"I will attempt to keep the blood to a minimum, Master

Boles," Berta said. She huffed when he only stared at her, a tiny smile flirting with the corners of his mouth. "Master, she is an industrial spy."

"Granted," Master Boles said so calmly that Berta couldn't help but glare at him for his casual attitude. "She's also your lover."

"That never made sense," Berta growled.

"Then why take her as your lover?" Master Boles asked. His curiosity seemed to be real if the raised eyebrow and raised chin were anything to judge by. "I hadn't thought you were interested in taking any lovers at all."

Berta snorted. Normally she wouldn't have answered the question at all. Most times when people asked such things Berta simply glared them into silence. Her sexuality and choices of partner were not for public discussion. Master Boles, however, owned not just her debt but also her loyalty. She had no intention of leaving his service except in a body bag.

"I expected a betrayal," Berta said. "Adalina is not the type to find me attractive despite her fetish for knives. Her behavior has been suspicious from the beginning."

"Then why indulge in the relationship...?" Master Boles raised both eyebrows, rotating his chair slightly as he waved for Berta to continue. He chuckled at the blush that suddenly stained Berta's cheeks. "That good, is she?"

Berta cleared her throat and squared her shoulders before nodding. "Yes, Master."

"Hmm, well, determine what her target was," Master Boles said, slipping back into the stern, implacable Master of business that everyone else saw. "Determine who her contacts are. And do attempt to keep the trauma to the support staff to a minimum, Berta. I'd rather not have to pay for more therapy for the first responders."

"Yes, Master," Berta said.

She saluted and turned smartly, striding out of the office. Jeff's office seemed like a sauna by comparison to the chill in Master Boles' room. When she strode in Jeff looked up and sighed. His smile was sympathetic, sad, but full of the sort of determination that made her approve of him. No matter that his heart was appallingly soft, he would do what was necessary to keep Master Boles and the rest of them safe.

"Where is she?" Berta asked.

"The main cafeteria," Jeff said, showing Berta his computer screen with the camera feed for the corner of the room Adalina was in. "I've begun researching everyone she's had contact with. Difficult given that she's in housekeeping. She goes everywhere and talks to everyone."

"I'll get you more data soon," Berta promised.

"Good luck," Jeff called as Berta strode out of the room.

Berta snorted. Luck had nothing to do with it. Adalina would reveal her secrets and then she would be handled as was appropriate to her crimes. Excellent orgasms were no reason for sentimentality. Adalina might have thought that her sexual prowess would protect her but she'd chosen the wrong target. No matter what it took Berta would discover the truth of Adalina's spying.

12:27 PM, THURSDAY

APRIL 1, 2012

Berta looked out over the cafeteria, doing her best not to glower from her post by the door to the kitchen. The beginning of each quarter was always a trial. Master Boles' newest debt slaves arrived in the morning, going through their initial orientation in the morning so that by lunch time they were prepared to start work.

Not that a large proportion of them would last very long. Master Boles' determinedly purchased only debt slaves who had either major performance problems. They were career criminals who could not be rehabilitated. Some were extremely brilliant individuals who had little clue how to behave as debt slaves. There were always problems.

The first three days were the worst. Someone always started a fight. Someone always attempted rape. Someone always broke down into hysterics in the middle of the cafeteria over nothing at all.

"Breathe," Josh murmured from the other side of the doorway.

"It's been too long," Berta growled at him. "Someone should have broken by now."

"You don't even have to be here," Josh sighed. "Seriously, ma'am, your highly ranked enough that you don't need to do this. You're not a guard anymore."

He winced when she glared at him, shrugged before turning to stare out at the cafeteria with a line of sweat running down one freckled, pale cheek. Berta snorted. Someday he might rise through the ranks but she suspected that Josh would end up in lower management rather than anywhere with true authority. No matter how many times she explained it, Josh never understood that there were some things one had to take care of oneself.

The break that she'd anticipated finally happened. A tiny woman with huge breasts screeched as one of the men sitting next to her suddenly grabbed her and hauled her into his lap. He tried to kiss the woman despite her efforts to push him away. Berta strode over, Josh by her side. Josh grabbed the woman out of the man's arms while Berta grabbed the hair on the back of the man's neck.

"The fuck?" the man gasped only to have his next words extinguished as Berta slammed his face into his tray of food.

Gravy smeared his face, mashed potatoes filling his nostrils when Berta pulled his head back up. There was no blood, as Berta had intended, and the man seemed only mildly disoriented, if quite startled by the attack. He attempted to brace his arms against the table to keep a repeat from happening but Berta was a foot taller and half a foot wider at the shoulders than he was. It wasn't going to work if she exerted herself.

"You okay?" Josh asked the woman who clung to him despite barely coming up to his breastbone.

"He, he wouldn't stop teasing," the woman gasped, shaking as tears ran down her cheeks. "Keeps following me around and he won't leave me alone!"

"Watch her," Berta snapped at Josh.

"She wanted it!" the man protested, his friends nodding with the excessively wide-eyed looks of feigned innocence.

"Be quiet," Berta snarled as she slammed his face back into the tray, this time much harder.

This time there was blood. His nose was properly broken. She'd aimed properly to split his lip on the ridge between the main dish compartment of his tray and the desert compartment. Mashed potatoes and gravy filled his left eye while pudding covered his right. Berta hauled him away from the table, adding a grip to his wrist when the man tried to flail at her.

"You can't do this!" one of his friends protested. "We got rights!"

"You were warned that nothing even hinting at rape was allowed," Berta snarled at them, gratified that all four of his friends went white and curled inwards at the sight of her anger. "This is well over the line. Learn from his example."

Berta wasn't surprised at all that the woman burst into tears. That gave them their hysterical collapse, as expected. She hauled the idiot away, ignoring his fumbling attempts to pull her hand out his hair. Behind her, Berta heard his friends start shouting only to be beaten down as the other guards in the cafeteria dealt with their nascent fight. And that made three.

The idiot turned out to be Anthony Johnson, convicted of identity theft and sentenced to debt slavery because of it. Jeff approved his summary sale with only three seconds of review of his file. His friends were dragged in as Berta left, each of them with vivid bruises blooming on their faces and bloody noses. Jeff and the little woman weren't there so Berta sought them out once she returned to the cafeteria.

To her surprise, Josh was back at his post but the woman was sitting on the floor next to him with her tray of food in her lap, back against the wall.

"She wanted to sit close to me," Josh said with a sheepish shrug.

"I just... wanted to be a little safer," the woman said with a quaver in her voice that made Berta fight to not curl her lip in disgust. "Sorry."

"You'll be fine, Adalina," Josh said. "In three days or so the bad apples will all have been sorted out and no one will bother you."

"Three days?" Adalina asked, staring up at Berta, not Josh, with curiosity and admiration in her eyes.

"The process generally takes between fifty-four and seventy-eight hours," Berta replied. "Master Boles specifically picks dead-end debt slaves in an effort to reform them."

Adalina's cheeks went flamingly red. She was appallingly plump, clearly one of those people who ate to deal with stress rather than working out to become stronger. With a blush her skin looked almost mahogany brown, nearly the same shade as her auburn hair. Berta didn't allow herself the snort that she wanted. The woman clearly took things entirely too personally.

"He also picks really bright people," Josh said with a mildly scolding look at Berta that got him a flat stare in return. He started sweating again. "We can't tell who's who at a glance though."

"Thanks," Adalina sighed as she carefully scraped up every morsel of food on her tray, even the remnants of her gravy. "But I suppose I could be considered one of the dead end ones. This is my second time through."

That was unusual enough that Berta and Josh both stared at her. She curled inward on herself as much as possible given the sheer size of her bust. It made her look considerably fatter than she actually was. Adalina licked her fork clean and then ran a finger around the edges of her tray's compartments as if searching for the tiniest fragments of food.

"The first time was my school debt," Adalina murmured just barely loud enough for Berta to hear her. "This time it's to pay off my mother's medical debt. She got cancer. The bills were... too much for them, especially since my dad's insurance refused to pay for the experimental therapy that saved her life. Sometimes I think I'll spend the rest of my life as a debt slave but at least my mom is alive, you know?"

Her earnest appeal was aimed at Berta, not Josh. Berta nodded while Josh made appropriately sympathetic noises. Berta let him take care of that. She would never understand the sort of filial devotion that other people felt for their families. If her mother came down with cancer, Berta would laugh and celebrate.

Around the cafeteria, the other debt slaves and employees began gathering their trays and mugs. Berta checked the time, nodding to herself as she ignored Josh's low-voiced sympathetic rendition of how he'd become a debt slave. Seven minutes and she could go back to her regular duties. Adalina cleared her throat as she stood, nodding to Josh before turning eyes that shone with gratitude and something very like flirtatious interest on Berta.

"Thank you for rescuing me," Adalina said, one leg cocked in that most submissive of female poses that canted the hips and emphasized the waist. "I appreciate it a lot. Really."

"It's my job," Berta replied entirely too coldly for the situation. "You'd best go. You'll be late."

Adalina stared at her, nothing but startlement in her eyes for a moment. Then anger flickered over her face followed by injured pride and a sort of rueful awareness that Berta had seen through her seductive stratagems. Josh made a strangled noise but he didn't say anything or make any inappropriate moves.

"I'd like to talk to you more," Adalina said only to Berta. "I mean, privately?"

"Personally," Berta clarified, allowing as much skepticism as she felt to come out in her voice. "As in, you're interested in me sexually, not him."

This time the strangled noise Josh made was something very similar to 'fuck my life' but Adalina ignored it just as Berta did. Adalina's blush returned and intensified until it crept up to her scalp, down her neck and out to the tips of her ears. She laughed a little breathlessly, shrugging one shoulder as she nodded once.

"Well, yes," Adalina admitted.

"Then don't act like that around me," Berta said. "I don't like it. Honesty matters to me."

Adalina grinned up at her, the smile so open and honest that Berta could see why Josh sighed as if he was a leaky tire. "I'll do that. Um, maybe dinner?"

"I'll be on guard duty for dinner," Berta said. "We can talk after that."

"It's a date," Adalina said.

She nodded to Josh and then hurried off to get rid of her tray. Berta sighed as she settled in to wait out the last few stragglers who always attempted to malinger over their meals instead of getting straight to work. Josh grumbled something that Berta didn't attempt to decipher. He stared out over the cafeteria as if he was trying to figure something out. He turned to stare at her two minutes, thirty-seven seconds later.

"How the hell do you do that?" Josh asked. "I comfort her and she leaps straight at you."

Berta smiled, turning to look at him. He went pale and started sweating again but he didn't look away. To her surprise, Josh held her eyes for a full thirty second. She chuckled and nodded approvingly.

"I tend to make a good first impression," Berta replied, allowing her smile to widen enough that teeth showed.

"Oh," Josh squeaked as he whipped his head around and returned to watching the stragglers in the cafeteria.

The sweat soaking his armpits and chest made Berta chuckle. No, Josh wouldn't rise too high in the security staff but he might do well supervising the new debt slaves. She would have to suggest it to Jeff and Master Boles when she saw them at the afternoon security meeting.

11:58 AM, WEDNESDAY

APRIL 28, 2012

"*A*da."

Berta allowed herself to smile, just a little one that barely quirked her lips. As predicted, Adalina gasped at having someone sneak up behind her. She whirled and then beamed at Berta. Now that she was paying attention properly, Berta could see how Adalina flicked through various responses as she turned, first fear, then anger, then a mockery of open delight that still left her posture highly guarded. Shoulders drawn in, feet set in carefully chosen positions that mimicked Berta's wide set stance without having the solid grounding that came from knowing how to defend herself.

"Berta!" Adalina exclaimed. "Goodness, you surprised me. Is anything wrong?"

"No," Berta said. "I talked to your supervisor. We're having lunch together in my rooms."

Instead of surprise or confusion, as Berta had never done this before and had said that she never would, Adalina's eyes showed a moment of suspicion before switching to flirtatious pleasure. Berta smiled just a little more widely, hooking her hands behind her back so that Adalina wouldn't see the way her fingers curled into claws. Even knowing what Berta knew about Adalina's first round of debt slavery, Berta found herself irritated at the artificial mannerisms.

"You're sure it's okay?" Adalina asked. "I don't want to get in trouble."

"Mm-hmm," Berta said. "I had news and wanted to celebrate."

"Oh," Adalina breathed.

She blinked four times, eyes just a hair too wide to be believable before cocking her head at Berta. Rather than saying what her 'news' was, Berta nodded for Adalina to push her housekeeping cart into the storage closet so that they could leave. As soon as they left, Berta's security team would be all over the thing, searching for any notes or hidden USB sticks that Adalina might have secreted on it.

Jeff hadn't been exaggerating when he said that Adalina had access to every part of the mansion and that she talked to everyone. Searching her cart and questioning her was very likely going to be the only way that Berta would find out who her contacts were other than torturing her.

The promise of torture had Berta's heart beating faster.

"Does that mean I can be a little bit late getting back to work?" Adalina asked.

"Your boss doesn't expect you back for the rest of the day," Berta said completely truthfully. If her smile was a little cold, hopefully Adalina would dismiss it. "I thought we might make a certain fantasy come true."

Adalina's eyes dilated dramatically as she swallowed convulsively. She stared at the large knife on Berta's hip. Berta smiled the same cold smile and Adalina's nipples abruptly poked through her shirt. Their slow walk towards Berta's quarters changed into a much more swift near-run with Adalina in the lead.

That, at least, was real.

It was gratifying to know that there was one true thing about her brief relationship with Adalina. As calculated as choosing Berta as her lover had to have been from Ada's point of view, she truly did have a fetish for knife play. Which was fine as far as Berta was concerned. It would certainly make getting Adalina naked for the coming interrogation much easier. Master Boles had requested that she minimize the amount of blood shed to be cleaned up, after all.

"Lunch?" Adalina asked, her voice coming out in a much higher register than normal. "Or um, play first?"

"I was thinking a shower first," Berta suggested as she tugged her collar open and started stripping her jacket off. "It's been a busy day for both of us and it has been a bit since you shaved."

Adalina's whine was so desperately aroused that Berta laughed. For the first time, she was truly enjoying flirting with Ada. Granted, Berta was well aware that what she and Ada thought of as flirting were two completely separate things. She was relatively certain that Adalina believed she would come through this afternoon with minimal damage. Berta was hoping for the exact opposite to happen.

"Shower sounds good," Adalina panted as she kicked off her shoes and stripped her clothes off rough and quick. "Very good. I'd like that. Please? Now?"

"Go get the water started," Berta said as she sat to remove her boots. "I'll be right in with my best knife."

The panties that Adalina slid off were already wet. She disappeared into the bathroom with another whimper that made Berta smile. Her reflection in the mirror looked vicious, nasty, cruel. No one else would have wanted to be in an enclosed space with Berta and her knives when she smiled that way. Adalina's lust had to be blinding her to the threat coming her way.

Once the water started running Berta went to the front door, letting the secondary security team in. They took Adalina's clothes and shoes, nodding respectfully to Berta before leaving with them. Anything on her clothes would now be searched and examined until all Adalina's secrets were revealed.

Berta stripped down to her skin. She hesitated over which knife to use but there really wasn't much of a choice. The smaller knives wouldn't do. Neither Adalina nor Berta would find them satisfying. Only her largest Bowie knife would suffice today. It had both the emotional impact that Adalina was looking for and the penetrating power and cutting edge that Berta wanted.

The bathroom was steamy when Berta walked in, steam turning the glass of the big shower stall semi-opaque. She couldn't see herself in the mirror but Berta didn't really care about that. Ada might be a bit disappointed not to see Berta coming but given the whimpers coming from the shower stall Berta suspected that Ada was entirely too horny to care about anything other than coming her brains out.

"Did I say you could play with that?" Berta asked as she slipped into the shower stall.

"N-no," Adalina gasped, pulling her fingers away from her clit with a visible effort. "Oh God. That's the big knife."

"Mm-hmm," Berta said. "Shut off the water and sit on the bench."

Adalina fumbled with the shower controls, turning it off without looking. Her eyes were locked on Berta's knife. She walked across the shower, brushing against Berta as she went, so that she could sit on the built-in bench on the far side of the shower. Berta had never had any interest in the bench until Adalina had become her lover. It was wasted work as far as she was concerned.

But it did make a lovely spot for Adalina to sit with her legs spread wide so that Berta had full access to her body. The O-ring set above the bench, supposedly for towels, was at exactly the right height for Adalina to grasp it. Three days after they'd gotten together Berta had put handcuffs on it. She snapped them around Adalina's wrists now.

"Better," Berta said as a surge of arousal made her belly heat. "I like having you restrained this way."

"Berta..." Adalina whimpered.

Her pupils had blown so wide that there was practically nothing left of the iris. Berta grinned as she knelt between Adalina's legs. This truly was going to be fun. It had been years since she'd been given permission to indulge her tastes to this degree. She had to wonder just how long it would take before Adalina realized that she was in trouble.

"Pity we don't have a way to restrain your legs so that you can't close them," Berta commented as she drew the edge of the blade along the inside of Adalina's ankle.

"Nnn!" Adalina whimpered. "M-may-be... maybe the stretcher bar? I'd, I'd like that. I would."

"You are so tempting," Berta crooned as she drew the blade across the instep of Adalina's foot.

This time she pressed just hard enough to break the skin. Three tiny drops of blood welled up only to melt away on Adalina's damp skin. Berta wouldn't have thought that Adalina was aware enough to notice it but she jerked and shouted; her voice loud and desperate in the confines of the shower.

"Please!" Adalina begged. "Please, please, please the bar, please Berta, please!"

Berta stood, her breath coming faster as the heat in her belly made everything more intense. Every drop of water around them glittered like diamonds. The salty-sweet smell of Adalina's arousal mixed with the faintest hints of blood as Berta licked the edge of her blade. One wet strand of dark hair had curled around the top of Adalina's heavy breast, outlining a path for Berta's knife to take in a couple of minutes.

"Have you been good?" Berta asked, her lip curling because she knew perfectly well that Adalina hadn't. They wouldn't be here if she had.

"Oh God, please!" Adalina sobbed. "I want... I want... Please!"

She kept her toes in exactly the same spot on the slippery tile but her hips thrust and rocked. Berta growled, nodding as she stepped out of the shower and into the other room. The spreader bar was more something to keep Berta from crushing Ada's head when she was between Berta's thighs but it would work just as well for Ada. The thick leather wouldn't like the shower's damp environment but then Berta fully intended there to be enough blood that the thing wouldn't be useful ever again.

"Mmm, that's nice," Berta said as she stepped back into the shower with the spreader bar and it's attached cuffs. "You haven't moved."

"No, no, I won't," Adalina panted. "Please, Berta. Please. Give it to me. Please. I'll do whatever you want!"

Berta chuckled as she attached the cuffs to Adalina's ankles. The bar was heavy enough that she knew that Ada would have a hard time kicking even in the most extreme of pain. It was made of a heavy steel pipe filled with lead, covered with leather that could take the most powerful of kicks. She smiled at Adalina once she was fully restrained.

"Don't worry," Berta told Adalina. "You'll get everything I have to give you and you absolutely will do exactly what I want."

17:57 PM, THURSDAY

APRIL 6, 2012

"You're late," Adalina commented as Berta strode up.

She'd been leaning against the wall outside of Berta's office for the last hour. Berta hadn't let Adalina into the room, hadn't given her a chair to sit on, hadn't done anything other than acknowledge that she was present when she arrived. Despite that, Adalina smiled brightly at Berta as she closed and locked her office door.

"There are reports that suggest Black is going to attack one of our factories," Berta said, growling a little in pure annoyance that the man had eluded so many attempts to capture and/or kill him.

"Do you think he really will?" Adalina asked, her eyes wide with manufactured awe and surprise.

"Stop that," Berta snapped at her. "I already reviewed your full file. Jeff shared it with me when you didn't stop pursuing me."

Adalina's dark skin abruptly went so pale that she went grey. She looked away, all the gentle, flirtatious mannerisms gone. In their place was a cold, frightened young woman who looked half a step away from gutting anyone who got too close. It was surprisingly refreshing.

"Why would you do that?" Adalina asked. She turned back and then started when she saw the approving smile on Berta's lips. "What?"

"I like that you better than the fake one you show to everyone else," Berta explained.

The dangerous air disappeared only to be replaced by total confusion. Adalina stared up at Berta, mouth open but nothing came out. Berta chuckled as she gestured for them to head up the hallway towards the smaller cafeteria. The big one would already be closed by this point but Berta knew that she could get dinner at the small one. It was always open for the security staff that filtered in at odd hours.

"That me?" Adalina asked.

"The one that's half a step away from causing mayhem," Berta said. "You looked cold, dangerous. I like that. I hate dealing with people who hide what they are, what they can do. It makes me want to cut them open to see what else they might be hiding."

"Oh," Adalina said so faintly that Berta glared at her.

To her surprise, Adalina looked far more aroused than she did frightened. Berta raised an eyebrow. Adalina blushed, smoothing her hands over the work apron she still wore. She'd been assigned to housekeeping almost immediately due to her having been a debt slave previously. Jeff and Master Boles had both agreed with Berta that any debt slave who had been owned by Mistress Felice Hong had to be handled with care.

Putting her anywhere that the public might interact with her was absolutely out. Giving her routine access to the computer systems was also a ridiculously stupid idea. None of them had been happy with the idea of giving her access to the food they ate so housekeeping was the logical result. At least with the debt slavery tracking chip embedded in her arm they were always aware of where Adalina was.

"What?" Berta asked.

"I... like knives," Adalina murmured.

"You like them."

Adalina nodded, her cheeks going red.

"Like them."

"Um, yes," Adalina said as she blushed harder and harder under Berta's stern gaze. "A lot."

"How much is 'a lot'?" Berta asked as they entered the small cafeteria and went to collect their trays.

Unsurprisingly, Adalina didn't answer the question. Instead she got food, apparently blindly as she ended up with spinach that Berta already knew that she hated along with her beef stroganoff. Berta waited, gathering her own food and then making sure that they ended up in the back corner of the room with Berta's back firmly to the wall and Adalina opposite her.

Adalina looked as though she fully intended to pretend that she'd never heard Berta's question. She poked at her spinach, squirming at the way the green mass clumped under her fork. Berta let her have the silence for as long as it took for her to efficiently eat her dinner. That took six minutes, by which point Adalina's shoulders had relaxed and she'd eaten around the spinach, leaving it entirely intact.

"How much is 'a lot'?" Berta asked as she sipped her water.

"What?" Adalina squeaked, staring at Berta with wide eyes that for once looked entirely honest. That sort of gaped mouth frightened expression rarely was the result of artifice.

"Knifes," Berta said. "How much is 'a lot' when talking about liking them? Is it a fetish? A kink? Something that you want to buy and enjoy? You want to make them someday?"

The questions embarrassed Adalina enough that she dropped her fork into the spinach so that she could hide her face with both hands. Berta smirked, enjoying the way Adalina whined. Getting through Adalina's determined efforts to seduce had taken quite some time so it was nice to finally see the actual person that existed underneath all the false mannerisms.

"So?" Berta prompted when Adalina didn't respond.

"Why do you need to know?" Adalina hissed. Her glare when she dropped her hands was nearly fierce enough to be believed.

"Fake," Berta said. She allowed her face to go completely flat.

"You... can tell," Adalina said, the fake anger disappearing into honest calculation and fear. "You've always been able to tell."

"I have a gift for it," Berta said in the sort of sarcastic drawl that usually made people shudder and draw away.

Around them, the other tables were mostly empty. One of the security guards was powering his way through his dinner, visibly trying not to listen in on their conversation. As soon as Berta drawled he shuddered and stood, carrying his tray to the opposite end of the room. No one else was close enough to overhear them, though of course the security cameras would record everything they said and did.

Berta was highly aware of that. Adalina didn't seem to be aware of anything other than Berta but she still snorted with amusement as she looked around them. The realization that they were as private as anyone ever got in Master Boles' mansion made Adalina's shoulders relax more than Berta had ever seen. The difference wasn't pronounced, just a quarter inch drop on either side coupled with a slight widening of her arms but it was significant.

"You always calculate your effect on others," Berta commented.

"Of course," Adalina huffed. "You said you'd seen my file."

"Prostitute or spy?" Berta asked.

Adalina glared, fierce, honest, completely true by every measure that Berta had. "Neither! I was support staff. Despite the tits I wasn't considered good enough for dealing with the public. And no one's supposed to know about the spying, anyway."

Berta laughed at that. Mistress Hong might think that she'd kept her industrial espionage secret but every major Master knew that she indulged in it. Of course they all did too. While Berta's job didn't involve working with the espionage agents, she knew that it occurred. It simply wasn't in her department. Master Boles' companies were as close as one could get to a military organization while actually being purely private commercial entities.

Her amusement made Adalina sigh and stare, annoyance open for Berta to see for the first time. It was a far more attractive expression that her studied mannerisms. Granted, it made the wrinkles at the edges of Adalina's eyes far more obvious and the creases alongside her mouth were much more prominent but Berta thought it suited her far better.

"Much better," Berta said. "Of course we know. All the major Masters know. All of them do it."

"I suppose," Adalina sighed.

"'A lot'?" Berta asked.

"Will you let that go?" Adalina complained. "I can't believe I said that! Just forget I said it, please."

"Why would I?" Berta asked. She laughed into her glass of water, amused by the sheer fury on Adalina's face. Open emotions suited her so much more. "How else am I to figure out if it's a matching fetish to mine?"

Fury disappeared, replaced by so much blatant arousal and need that Berta didn't need an answer. She'd seen that expression on her own face the last time she'd gotten to torture a man to death. Certainly, Adalina probably wasn't going to volunteer to be cut up like a Christmas turkey but she very clearly liked the idea of knives far more than a mere kink.

"Knives," Berta said. "Can you actually come without them being involved?"

"N-not usually," Adalina whispered. The blush this time had more to do with her nipples poking through and the way she panted with arousal than it did with embarrassment. "You…?"

"We should go somewhere private so that we can talk," Berta said. She set her glass down on her tray before standing. "Now?"

"Oh God, yes please," Adalina groaned. "Please!"

12:18 PM, WEDNESDAY

APRIL 28, 2012

"Stay still," Berta growled as she dragged her knife up Adalina's inner thigh.

The shuddering breath that Adalina drew in wasn't half as exciting as the trail of blood drops Berta's knife left behind as she scored a long thin line exactly where she'd cut later to debone Adalina's leg. There were a dozen marks already, each so shallow that they barely broke the skin. Two arched across the tops of Adalina's breasts. One cut across the curve of her belly, intersecting her bellybutton before continuing downwards towards her now-shaved groin.

Adalina had a dozen little nicks, places where Berta had 'slipped' and broken the skin. She hadn't figured the situation out yet, much to Berta's amusement. So far it was all sex and nothing else to Adalina. It wouldn't last too much longer. Berta knew how long her teams would require to thoroughly search Adalina's cart, clothes and rooms. The amount of time it would take to isolate anyone that she'd talked to repeatedly over the last month was finite. Her time was running out.

Berta couldn't wait to finally be free to play as she always wanted and so rarely got to. Granted, only Berta thought of it as play but that hardly mattered in this situation. Master Boles had given her permission to question Adalina. He'd all but said that blood was fine as long as she kept the mess reasonably under control.

It didn't get more controlled than keeping it in the shower stall. She probably should have known better than to do the last interrogation on her bed. The mess had been quite horrific by the time she was done. Today she would do better. And hopefully, if she kept herself under control, Master Boles would grant her the right to interrogate other people who were fundamentally expendable.

Adalina whined as Berta cut a long line along her inner arm, digging it in exactly shy of the artery. "Berta…!"

Berta glanced towards the clock on the counter, smiling as she saw that she was past time to begin working on Adalina. "Yes?"

"Sharp," Adalina gasped.

"Very," Berta agreed.

She dug the tip of the knife in, drawing the blade back so that it cut deeper into Adalina's arm. Berta couldn't go too deep here. The risk of hitting the artery was too high, not to mention the fact that it was much better to work bottom up than top down in situations like this. But she couldn't resist changing the dynamic now that it was time to start the real play.

"Ow!" Adalina squawked. "Too deep."

"Too bad," Berta said as she made an inch long cut about half an inch deep in Adalina's arm.

When she transferred the blade to the upper curve of Adalina's breast, the arch of her right foot over the spreader bar so that Ada couldn't kick, something about the cut or maybe it was the tone of Berta's voice finally got through to Ada. She stopped breathing despite Berta cutting another inch long groove in her ample breast.

"Berta?" Adalina asked, voice tiny and afraid for the first time since they'd become lovers. "What's wrong?"

Berta smiled into Adalina's eyes, deepening the cut until Adalina panted with pain instead of arousal. The difference was delicious. Ada shivered convulsively, fingers twisting and legs thrashing against the spreader bar without making the slightest bit of difference. Her protean gasps were rough and ragged, full of strangled noises that perfectly matched the terror filling her wide eyes.

"Did you really think you could get away with it for long?" Berta asked as she moved the knife to Adalina's other breast. "We're not fools, Ada. I'm not a fool. I always knew you were up to something. The only question was what and who your contacts are."

"Oh God," Adalina gasped.

This time Berta cut around the wide dark circle of Adalina's nipple, deliberately scoring deep enough that there was little likelihood that the bit of flesh would be saved even if Adalina survived. Blood dripped down Adalina's arm, along the curve of her other breast. The cut on her nipple bled down the curve of Berta's blade, dripping off the guard to spatter on Adalina's thigh.

"Please don't," Adalina begged. "Please. Berta, please! I can explain. Really! Berta!"

Her voice got higher and higher as Berta continued cutting in a deep spiral around her left breast. Berta shivered at the terror Adalina gave her. She still wasn't completely honest. There was too much calculation in what she said, how she said it. No matter. Berta would break her defenses entirely and then she would learn what they needed to know.

"You lie," Berta crooned as her spiral cut met up with the one that arched across Adalina's chest. It was exactly where an autopsy scar would go. "Why should I believe anything you say, Ada? You've lied nearly every time we spoke to each other. You lie in bed. You lie at work. You lie all the time. Master Boles doesn't like liars. Neither do I."

"I'm not lying!" Adalina shouted.

She tried to kick, tried to squirm free of the handcuffs. Surprisingly, she automatically dislocated her thumbs and very nearly succeeded in getting her hands free. Berta grinned as she slapped a hand around Adalina's wrist and tightened the cuffs to the point where they cut into Ada's flesh.

Adalina glared. This time she tried to get a foot free from the cuffs but it wasn't going to work. Berta laughed. The cuffs were too tight around her ankles, secured in place with the really secure sort of latch that took two hands and a good grip to get loose. It was obvious from Adalina's fury that she didn't believe that Berta would really hurt her.

"Oh, I knew you'd be fun in the end," Berta crooned as she carved an inch long cut along the back of Adalina's right calf. "It's been so long since I got to play for real. I knew from our second week that you'd be mine to play with in time."

Rather than replying, Adalina screamed. It was the sort of scream that usually brought people running, that made heads whip around to make sure that everything was all right. Even so, it didn't hold the right note of terror for Berta's taste so she added a second cut just above the first on Ada's calf.

This time the scream was pained, higher pitched and lovely but still not right. Berta switched to Adalina's left calf, carving a cut that matched beautifully with the first one. Adalina jerked and started screaming in earnest as she jerked against the handcuffs and ankle cuffs. After Berta carved a second cut on Ada's left calf she settled back to watch Adalina bleed for her.

It took nearly two full minutes before Adalina stopped screaming. She stared towards the bathroom door, eyes going wider and wider as she realized that no one was coming. Berta laughed, her heart beating so much faster that she had to bring her free hand down to her clit. A firm pinch made Berta shiver with pleasure, anticipation, satisfaction. Oh yes, this was going to be wonderful.

"They aren't coming," Adalina whispered.

"No, they're not," Berta agreed.

"Master Boles said…" Her terror was so much more perfect as she turned back to stare at Berta.

"This isn't rape, at least not officially," Berta drawled, her amusement powerful enough that she chortled at the way Adalina shook her head. "I'm a sexual sadist, Ada. I get off on torturing people. Master Boles knows that. He keeps me on a tight leash, only letting me play when he decides someone's a danger to his organization. You're a danger. You're a spy. You tried to steal information on his business. That means you're mine to play with for as long as I want, in whatever ways I want, until I get honest information."

This time when Berta brought her knife up to lick the blood off Adalina screamed exactly right. She lost bladder control as her scream spiraled higher and higher and her arms flailed against the handcuffs holding her in place. More blood dripped down her arms as she tore the skin on her wrists to shreds in an effort to get away from the predator she only just realized that she'd been fucking for a month.

Berta wrapped her free hand around Adalina's throat, squeezing until the scream turned into a wheezing gasp coupled with tears spilling down her cheeks. Oh yes, this was going to be one of the good ones. Instead of begging, Adalina glared at Berta while mouthing 'fuck you'.

"You already did, Ada," Berta whispered. She bent to press a kiss against Adalina's lips, laughing as Ada tried to bite. "Now it's my turn. Do try and last a while before you break. I want to enjoy this as much as possible."

15:03 PM, THURSDAY

APRIL 11, 2012

"No," Berta said, glaring at Adalina.

"But why?" Adalina whined.

It was one of the truly honest whines, not an artificial one designed to elicit pity without annoying. Frankly, the tenor of Adalina's voice grated so badly that Berta was tempted to break her neck on principle. Apparently, her anger showed because Adalina looked away, smoothing her hands over her thighs.

"I don't let anyone else handle my knives," Berta replied. "Ever. I don't care if you think it would be a turn-on or not. You're not touching my knives, Ada. If you want to play like that then you'll buy your own knife and bring it to the bedroom."

"I'm not allowed to buy them," Adalina complained.

She flopped back on Berta's bed dramatically with her arms flung over her head. The move made her round belly look flatter but her breasts sagged to the sides. It said something about how frustrated she was that she didn't hug them to keep them pointing in the 'right' direction. Berta relaxed a little just seeing the natural pose.

Working for Mistress Hong in her brothels had done terrible things to Adalina. Berta could count on one hand the number of times she'd seen Adalina behave and speak perfectly naturally, with no artifice at all. The woman she revealed at those times was fascinating enough to make up for the irritation of her sweet little sex kitten mannerisms the rest of the time.

Berta straddled Adalina's hips, smiling down at her scowl. "Too bad then. You'll just have to find other ways to get off, Ada."

"If I could, I would," Adalina complained. "You've seen. I need to have knives around, preferably pressing against me, to be able to come. It's so frustrating that no one understands that."

"Except me," Berta murmured as she bent to kiss Adalina.

Adalina bit her lip and tongue, arms still lying limply over her head. Berta chuckled and kissed her way down Adalina's naked body. The gentle touches weren't at all what either of them wanted. Over the last eleven days Berta had learned exactly how to push Adalina to the point that she stopped faking her pleasure and started demanding it. That was what she wanted today.

"Harder!" Adalina groaned as Berta kept laying feathery little touches around the mound of Adalina's belly. "Damn it, you could at least bite me!"

"Why would I want to do that?" Berta asked.

"You are such a fucking sadist," Adalina complained.

She squirmed, her fingers finally curling into claws that made Berta grin. A delicate, far too gentle touch against Adalina's inner thigh made her shout angrily. Berta laughed as Adalina grabbed her arm and hauled against her, trying to force her up on the bed.

"Move, move, move!" Adalina snapped. "Damn it, why do you insist on this stupid game?"

"I like teasing you," Berta replied.

She leaned back against the headboard with her legs spread wide. The grin made her cheeks hurt but it was well worth it when Adalina snarled at her. Instead of gentle touches and feathery kisses, Adalina stabbed two fingers into Berta's pussy, immediately curling them up to thrust against her G-spot. Ada bit the inside of Berta's thigh as she did it, sucking hard to leave a dark mark that would ache under Berta's pants.

"Better," Berta crooned.

"Bitch," Adalina grumbled as she bit Berta's clit. "Such a bitch!"

Her fingers pressed hard enough to make Berta gasp. The pain was pleasure, pure pleasure that made Berta's breath catch and her toes curl into the covers. Adalina's bites and vicious sucking on Berta's clit only added to the pleasure. No matter what Adalina looked like, she was nearly as sadistic as Berta.

Berta watched as Adalina's hips started thrusting against the air in time with her fingers' thrusting into Berta's pussy. It would be better to have a knife to Adalina's throat, for there to be the stink of blood and urine in the air. She groaned at the mental image of Adalina with blood dripping from multiple wounds all over her body. Adalina echoed her groan when Berta caught her hair and forced her face more firmly into Berta's groin.

"Bite!" Berta ordered.

"Mmmn!" Adalina moaned as she followed the order, grip of Berta's hands in her hair.

It didn't take long before Berta was making more noise than Adalina normally. She could almost smell the blood, Adalina's blood. If only she could pull out her knives and cut into Adalina's flesh. Berta trembled on the edge of a truly massive orgasm as she imagined watching Adalina's breath go to desperate gasps, her mouth dropped open and eyes going dull. Blood would have pooled underneath her, warm and sticky in all the best ways.

"Yes!" Berta shouted as she came from the thought of kissing Adalina's cooling lips.

She collapsed back against the pillows, legs trembling in the aftermath of her orgasm. It took several tugs before Berta let Adalina's hair go. Perhaps someday she'd get to have that pleasure again but for now she could imagine it. Berta smiled at the pride on Adalina's face. Her smile looked decidedly smug.

"Are you sure you won't let me lick one of your knives while you fuck me?" Adalina asked just hopefully enough for Berta to snicker.

"No, I won't," Berta said. "But I will fuck you with my big Bowie knife."

To Berta's amusement Adalina's smug pride immediately disappeared into lust. Her hands went straight to her groin, thrusting up into her pussy with the sort of desperation that Berta found most attractive short of bloodshed. Adalina panted as she stared at Berta, fingers so busy between her thighs that Berta laughed out loud.

"Why imagine it when I can make it happen?" Berta asked.

"The hilt?" Adalina asked as she licked her lips and thrust even deeper into her pussy.

"Mmm, I was thinking the sheathe," Berta said. "It's pretty snug on the knife. I should be able to slide it into you without much effort at all. I don't *think* that there will be any mistakes with the sheathe sticking while the knife comes out but you wouldn't mind a little nick here or there, would you?"

Adalina shouted, her head flung back in as obvious of an orgasm as Berta had ever seen. She collapsed on the bed, shaking as hard as Berta had been a few moments before.

When Berta pulled Ada's hands away from her groin, Berta could see that she was already starting to swell a little bit.

"Tsk," Berta said as she spread Adalina's legs for her. "Now you're swelling. More chance of a mistake happening."

"Oh God," Adalina whimpered. "Please do it! Please, Berta. Please!"

Berta rolled off the bed and went to get several of her knives. The big Bowie knife probably wouldn't work, in reality. She didn't have permission to cut Adalina. Even if Ada would say yes, Master Boles wouldn't. He'd made it perfectly clear that she wasn't to indulge in any cutting during knife play no matter how tempting the prospect might be.

Of course, this wasn't cutting. If there chanced to be a few small nicks that happened accidentally during their play that was a completely different thing from deliberately carving Adalina up. The only logical choices for this play were her second and third favorite knives. Berta's tanto had a very nicely fitted sheathe, solid wood that had been polished to a lovely gleam. It wouldn't slip unless Berta wanted it to. The shape was very similar to a dildo as well though Berta thought that Adalina would prefer something that was more obviously knife-shaped.

Her hawk-billed gutting knife was a bit wide for Adalina's pussy but it would give her exactly what she was looking for. It might even please Adalina, too. The pull and push of the knife into Adalina promised to loosen the sheathe just enough that an 'accident' was almost inevitable. Berta carried both the tanto and the hawk-billed gutter back to the bed, grinning at the way Adalina moaned.

"Yes, too swollen for the Bowie," Berta said as she stared at Adalina's glistening labia. "Two choices. Tanto or hawk-billed."

She let Adalina take the tanto first, not surprised at all that she immediately tested to see how tight the sheathe was.

Adalina grunted at the effort it took to glimpse an inch or so of the razor sharp blade. When she passed that back and tested hawk-bill Adalina whined. Berta watched Adalina argue silently with herself for the sanity of the tanto versus the riskiness of the hawk-bill.

Any average person would have gone with the tanto. It was sheer insanity to go with the hawk-bill and its wide blade, looser sheathe and longer, more wicked cutting edge. Berta knew which one she wanted: the hawk-bill. The only question in her mind was just how strong Adalina's fetish for knives really was.

"Can... Can we use the hawk-bill?" Adalina asked, her voice shaking as hard as her legs. "Will it fit? The sheathe is kind of rough."

"It'll fit," Berta crooned as she set the tanto aside and reached for the lube in the bedside table's drawer. "You'll just feel it for days."

"That one then, please," Adalina moaned. "Fuck me hard, Berta! Please!"

18:51 PM, WEDNESDAY

APRIL 28, 2012

Berta hummed as she washed her hair. It had taken quite some time, over six hours in fact, but Adalina finally broke. The damage was extensive but Berta had kept the injuries minor enough that Adalina should live. Probably.

Frankly, Berta was quite surprised that Ada had survived the questioning process once she had broken. She was tempted to take a very long time with her shower just so that Adalina would bleed out in the interim but Master Boles wouldn't approve of that. The girl had survived so that was that. Maybe next time Berta would be luckier. Frankly, by the time Berta had all the information she needed from Adalina, it looked as though Adalina was deep into subspace despite the terror and her many injuries.

"Please…"

The little whimper was exhausted enough that Berta laughed. She turned around and smiled down at what was left of Adalina. Her wrists were still caught in the handcuffs, the fingers rather blue from having been raised for so long.

Adalina's hair had gotten in the way about halfway through the process of breaking her so Berta had shaved it off.

That, of course, had led to cuts on her cheeks and lips, beautiful little patterns of slashes that barely broke the skin radiating down her chin and across the delicate skin of her neck. Those heavy breasts would more than likely have to be removed. Berta hadn't been gentle with them but then Adalina had earned the damage with her kicking, spitting and cursing.

Her stomach was covered with a snowflake pattern of cuts that slowly oozed blood. The entire floor of the shower was bloody. Berta smiled, deeply satisfied with the way it made her bathroom smell. Yes, the next time she had an interrogation she definitely would have to do it in the shower. If she was really lucky then the grout between the tiles would change color, giving Berta a lovely trophy from today's activities.

"Just a little clean up and then I'll call my crew," Berta told Adalina.

"I told... you..." Adalina whispered. "Please..."

"Mmm-hmm," Berta chuckled. "In time."

Freeing Adalina's hands from the cuffs made her pass out, probably because Berta was anything but gentle about it. The spreader bar was certainly ruined. Berta leaned that in the far corner of the shower stall, out of the way. Sometime in the next few weeks she'd have to replace it. Maybe if she paid enough she could get it recovered with fresh leather. That would be another trophy to enjoy if it was possible. The central steel pipe with its lead should be salvageable.

She used the shower wand to wash the majority of Adalina's blood away. It wasn't completely effective, of course. Adalina was still bleeding. But it did reduce the amount of blood her crew would be exposed to and hopefully it would be good enough to keep the first responders from running out to vomit in the hallway.

Berta took care to dry her feet so that she wouldn't leave bloody footprints on the carpet. Pulling her pants on was necessary, as was putting on a tank top so that she wouldn't flash her crew. Then she opened the door and smiled at the people waiting for her.

The medics looked as though they expected Berta to be covered in blood and gore from head to toe. They had a stretcher and all the gear they might need, including a body bag. Berta nodded at them respectfully before stepping aside so that they could enter.

"In the bathroom," Berta said. "In the shower. She's still alive and able to talk but she will need surgery fairly quickly."

"Fuck," Kari, the lead medic, cursed. "What the hell did you do to her?"

"I got the information Master Boles wanted without killing her," Berta snapped, more than a little annoyed at the woman. "You'll probably have to do a double mastectomy but that's her fault, not mine. She could have answered the questions instead of fighting. She didn't."

Kari waved to her team. They pushed past Berta, heading straight for the bathroom. Gale, her second in command, sighed and shook his head at Kari's teams as their curses and gagging sounded from the other room. He went to look, head cocked to the side as he saw how little blood there was.

"You cleaned up," Gale commented.

"Master Boles specifically requested that I not traumatize any more first responders," Berta explained.

"Nice work," Gale said as Kari and her team hauled Adalina's limp body out of the shower and put her onto the stretcher. He ignored Kari's worried chatter with her crew about IV's, blood transfusions and 'massive trauma'. "She should come through it fairly well."

Berta nodded. It would have been so much more satisfying to kill Adalina, to watch the blood drain out and her eyes go lifeless and dull but Master Boles had mentioned putting Adalina on computer duty so she had to presume he wanted her alive. Hopefully the next time Adalina betrayed them Master Boles would give her clear permission to kill her however she wanted.

"There's a fair amount of tendon damage on her legs and of course her breasts are probably a loss," Berta agreed. "But she should be able to function after proper medical care."

"Move!" Kari snapped at Gale and Berta.

They moved aside so that Kari and her team could rush Adalina out into the corridor and away to whatever medical intervention they deemed appropriate. A cleaning team hovered outside the door, looking so apprehensive that Berta sighed and went to put on her boots. Gale smiled wryly and shrugged.

"Anything you want to keep?" Gale asked.

"I'd love to see if my stretcher bar can be saved," Berta said. "The leather is ruined but I'm hopeful that it can be stripped and replaced. The core should still be good."

"I'll take care of it personally," Gale said with a nod of comprehension. "Jeff wanted to take down your deposition personally. He's waiting for you in his office."

"Good," Berta said. "Don't let them play with my knives."

"No, ma'am," Gale said. "Good job."

"We'll see whether it's effective in plugging any security holes," Berta sighed as she stood. "Keep watch until I'm back."

He saluted as Berta strode out of her quarters. It was a pity that she couldn't spend more time enjoying the scene but her memory was good. She'd be able to bring it all back whenever she wanted. Debriefing with Jeff took several hours, by which point Adalina was out of surgery. Master

Boles made a point of stopping by at the end of her deposition to praise how little damage Berta had done.

"There will be quite a lot of scarring," Master Boles said with a small frown, "but she'll survive with only minimal loss of function in her legs. The wrists are a bit of a mess but that was clearly caused by her struggles against the handcuffs."

Berta nodded. "She didn't stop fighting them until almost the end. Is there anything else, Master?"

Master Boles paused and stared at Berta with such a complicated, confusing expression that Berta had no clue what the problem was. From the puzzled tilt of Jeff's head, he couldn't figure it out either. After several seconds that made Berta straighten her spine until she was standing at attention, Master Boles sighed.

"She called for you as soon as she woke," Master Boles said. "And kept calling for you as she recovered from the anesthesia. You might want to visit."

"Downstairs?" Berta asked.

"We transferred her back here once she was stable enough to move." Master Boles nodded.

"Then I'll go now," Berta said. "No reason to wait."

She headed for the door only to stop when Master Boles cleared his throat. He looked troubled enough that she turned to face him once more. Jeff smoothed out his paperwork, fingers shaking slightly just as they had since Berta started her deposition.

"Was it Hong?" Master Boles asked.

"It was," Berta confirmed. "I got the access codes for several accounts that Adalina was taking payments through. You'll want to deal with Neal in Finance. He's apparently her main contact. She's not the only one, just the sloppiest one."

Master Boles growled, nodding for Berta to leave so that he could review her deposition with Jeff. Berta left, fairly certain that they would have yet another round of discussions on how Master Boles could keep an obvious serial killer on staff. She had no idea of the content of those discussions having made a point of not reviewing the security recordings whenever they started one.

It didn't matter, Berta thought as she took the elevator down to the infirmary. Master Boles had uses for her. She was a valuable member of his team. And occasionally, often enough to satisfy that part of her soul that screamed for blood and death, she got to use her less socially acceptable skills in ways that she enjoyed. That was enough for Berta to be happy serving Master Boles.

Adalina was laying, pale and covered in bandages, on the bed farthest from the door. The curtain hadn't been drawn around her bed but it didn't really need to be. The infirmary was empty of patients other than Adalina. Kari was the only medic there. She sat at her desk, filling out paperwork while snarling as if she was so pissed off that she wanted to tear people apart.

"She keeps calling for you," Kari grumbled as soon as Berta walked in. "What the hell did you do to her?"

"I would think you saw what I did," Berta said as she headed for Adalina's bed.

Berta watched Adalina sleep for a few moments. Most of the damage was hidden behind the bandages that covered her body but Berta knew exactly what was under each one. Adalina's chest was flat. The bountiful breasts that had distracted so many people were gone. It was an improvement as far as Berta was concerned. The best part, the part that made heat bloom in his stomach again, was the Berta had done that. It was a permanent change to Adalina's body, something that would forever remind her of what Berta had done.

When Adalina opened her eyes and saw Berta standing at the foot of her bed she jerked in automatic terror. The terror faded almost immediately, replaced but the sort of lust that had marked the beginning of the interrogation. Berta raised an eyebrow at Adalina as Ada licked her cut lips and winced. Lust was an unexpected result from today's activities. Apparently she'd underestimated Adalina's knife fetish.

"Again," Adalina whispered.

"What?" Berta asked, surprised enough that her voice easily carried to Kari's desk.

"Do it... again..." Adalina repeated, her voice thready but determined.

Kari stood, her expression stern and horrified. She might not have heard exactly what Adalina had said but she could probably read Berta's smug body language easily enough. As Berta chuckled, low and evil, Kari strode over with her hands hooked into claws.

"I don't have permission to do it again," Berta said.

Adalina whined. Her eyes went narrow and angry only to go wide with a sudden realization. She smiled, winced at the way her cut lips started bleeding again and then nodded as if she'd just figured out how to get everything she ever wanted. Berta snorted, taking a little jar of lip balm from the bedside table. Smoothing more of it over Adalina's lips made her shiver and moan.

"Betray Master Boles again and I'll just gut you," Berta told Adalina despite Kari's squawk of dismay. "There won't be any play, Ada."

"Then kill me," Adalina huffed. "I don't want to live if I can't have that again!"

Kari grabbed Berta's arm, hauling her away from the bed. She stood between them, glaring at Berta as if it was all her fault instead of Adalina's. Berta ignored Kari, focusing entirely on Adalina's expression. It slid from angry to flirtatious to frustrated and then back into a sort of rising fear that made Berta remember the smell of blood and urine in her shower.

"I don't have permission to kill you, Ada," Berta drawled despite Kari's determined efforts to throw her out of the infirmary. "Too bad. I would have enjoyed doing it. You were lovely as you bled out for me."

"Get out!" Kari bellowed at Berta. "You fucking psycho, get the hell out of my infirmary!"

"I'm not psychotic, Kari," Berta said with a little sniff. "I'm just a product of my upbringing. Don't betray Master Boles again, Ada. He's not likely to give me a second round with you."

Both Kari's gasp of horror and Adalina's wail of outrage followed Berta out into the hallway. She laughed as Kari started cursing over the top of Adalina's wails. It wasn't as good as an actual murder but it was still a lovely day's work. Berta hummed as she headed back upstairs to her rooms. Hopefully tomorrow would be just as good of a day as today had been.

"Ah," Berta sighed as she rode the elevator up towards her floor. "What a wonderful evening."

The End

AUTHOR'S NOTE: SILKEN EMBRACE

In contrast to Controlled Edge, Silken Embrace is a mostly fluffy story. Not that many stories in this 'verse are ever truly 100% fluffy but Silken Embrace comes close. At the very least this one has laughter and cuddles to go with the kink and dubious consent.

1. MISSION PROTOCOL

"So who is she?" Tommy asked as they all did last minute fixes on their makeup and clothes.

It was weird wearing makeup. Granted, there wasn't much, just a bit of bubblegum pink gloss on his lips and a hint of shadow on his eyes that played up the blue of his irises but it was still more than he'd ever worn. The gel that made his mousy brown hair stand up in artistic spikes had darkened his hair slightly even in the garishly bright lights of the dressing room. Every single one of them had blue eyes, pale skin and brown hair. Tommy was pretty sure that was a deliberate choice on Mistress Hong's part.

"Mistress Teolinda Horne," Annie said as she fussed with the curls cascading down her shoulder. "Fourth richest and most powerful person in the state, sixth most powerful east of the Mississippi."

She shifted on her hard plastic stool, angling to get the best view of how her hair looked on her back. The dressing room was anything but elegant. The bare white walls were scuffed and cracked and the floor had ripples where the linoleum had been put down incorrectly. Huge racks of lingerie stood against the far walls, all of it shared between the debt slaves who worked in this brothel. Granted, it was all beautifully made but it was strange not having clothes of his own to wear.

Tommy had been a little appalled when he arrived here to discover that he wouldn't have clothes to wear during his downtime. Clothes were for working or the rare occasions he was allowed out in public. Most of the time they were expected to be nude. At least the brothel was kept warm enough that skin was comfortable. Honestly, even his outfit tonight felt a little too warm though it wasn't bad enough to make him sweat.

It was one of the few comfortable things about his new life. Just like Annie's stool, everything outside of the play rooms and public lobby was hard, cheap and made to last. No efforts were made to make their lives more comfortable. The windowless little dressing room was no different from the rest of the 'private' areas of the brothel: hard, bare and completely unadorned. A few favorites of Mistress Hong got better beds and more food but that still wasn't what they would have gotten if they were free. Tommy hadn't objected to the lack of privacy or clothes. Doing so seemed like a sure way to get in trouble.

"Likes silk and corsets," Jerry agreed as he carefully tugged his corset down over his hips, smoothing it with an absent frown. "Enjoys the new kids more than the more established ones. No really violent kinks but she'll make you work for your orgasm. The more obvious you can be about enjoying her kinks the more she'll get into it and the more she'll reveal."

"She'll pick you," Lena said. She pressed her lips together over a tissue and then nodded as she applied a sealer gloss on top of the bright red lipstick. "You're cute, young and exactly her type, Tommy. Just give her what she wants and it'll go well."

None of them were in proper clothes. Tommy had scarlet hot pants that were so tight that he could barely sit down with a deeper red silk tank top that was translucent enough to show off the new nipple rings. He'd gotten them once his physical training started despite his protests that he didn't want any piercings.

The medic who'd done the piercing had shrugged away his objections and had Tommy held down for the procedure. Apparently, Mistress Hong had ordered it herself so Tommy's objections didn't matter. His nipples still ached a bit but not enough that anyone cared. They were healed enough that he could touch them and they wouldn't get infected. That was enough as far as Mistress Hong and her medical staff was concerned.

Annie's frilly little slip dress was burgundy, made of gauze that let you see everything. Lena's strapless dress covered her the most but it was so tight that she hadn't even bothered trying to sit down. If she had, Tommy was pretty sure that it would have split open at the seams. Jerry's corset was coupled with a G-string that was more obscene than being naked.

"You're sure she'll pick me?" Tommy said. He could see how frightened he looked in the mirror. None of the others made any attempt to reassure him other than a casual shrug from Lena that nearly popped her nipples out of her dress.

"Yeah," Jerry said, still frowning at his reflection and fussing with the corset. "You're exactly what she looks for."

"Don't worry about it," Annie said, flapping a hand at Tommy. "She gives huge tips even if you don't completely satisfy her. She'll dress you up and fuck you silly and it'll be okay."

They all stood at attention as Mistress Hong came in, two

huge burly guards at her back. She was tiny, her Asian ancestry a mix of South Pacific and Japanese that had given her a flat nose, narrow lips and slender eyes that glared even when she wasn't angry. Tommy had yet to see Mistress Hong when she wasn't angry. Even in four inch heels she barely came up to Tommy's breastbone. The ferocity of her scowl made him shiver. That was the sort of expression that led to beatings back home, especially when his father had been drinking.

He hadn't heard of Mistress Hong beating anyone bloody but he already knew better than to cross her. Before he'd gotten transferred to a different bunk, Urith had filled Tommy in on all the ways that life could suck if you didn't please Mistress Hong. She rarely punished them directly but Urith had told Tommy the sort of horrible duties he might end up with if he failed to perform as required. Mistress Hong glared at them all, shaking her head at Jerry's corset before nodding approval at the rest of them.

"No corsets," Mistress Hong snapped. "Take it off and put on a robe or something, Jerry. Make it the long blood red robe, the one with velvet cuffs. Don't tie it up."

"Yes, Mistress," Jerry said as he hurriedly started unlacing the corset. "Sorry, Mistress."

Annie helped him so that they'd be ready in time. Tommy would have too but Mistress Hong came over to stare up at him. It felt like she was trying to peel his skin off from the sheer intensity of her gaze. About the time Jerry unhooked his corset, Mistress Hong nodded.

"She'll pick you," Mistress Hong said. "The rest of you will report for secondary duties after the selection process. It's a busy night tonight. On the off chance that she doesn't pick Tommy, listen up."

Jerry shrugged into the silk robe, coming back to stand at

attention next to Annie, Lena and Tommy. Behind her, the two guards snapped to attention too. Tommy wondered wildly for a second if they were supposed to pay attention or if it was just habit, protective coloring so that Mistress Hong wouldn't get mad at them if she glanced their way.

"Teolinda won't talk about her business," Mistress Hong said with the sort of snarl that suggested that she found that enormously irritating. "I already have spies in her command structure so that hardly matters. What I want to know is who her new lover is. She broke up with her last lover a month ago and took someone new this week. I need to know who it is so that I can get an angle on them. Your mission is to get me that name or at least a description of the person. Any information about her lover is better than none but I want that name."

She stabbed one long perfectly manicured nail into Tommy's chest. He gulped and nodded, not even trying to hide the way he shivered. No one else in the room so much as twitched so Tommy nodded again as he drew in a shaky breath.

"Yes, Mistress," Tommy said. His voice quivered as much as his knees.

"Good," Mistress Hong said. "Now get a grip and calm down. She'll be here any minute."

Mistress Hong strode out, the guards following her. One of them looked sympathetically at Tommy but he didn't say a word. Once the door shut Tommy groaned. The temptation to rub his face and run his fingers through his hair was enormous but he didn't want to mess up his makeup or the gel in his hair.

Lena chuckled, patting Tommy's shoulder. "You'll be fine. Really. Mistress Teolinda is a sweet woman and she talks pretty freely about her love life."

"I guess," Tommy said, running his hands over his thighs for the lack of anything better to do. "It's just the first time I've had to do this for real. I don't want to mess up."

"Don't ask her anything outright," Jerry advised.

"Definitely not!" Annie agreed. "Maybe after you guys fuck do that little pouty thing you do when you're feeling sad, the one with the puppy eyes and bottom lip, and sigh about missing your girlfriend back home."

"I ah, don't have a girlfriend back home," Tommy said as his cheeks heated. He hadn't realized that he was that obvious.

"Boyfriend, then," Annie said, waving the objection away. "If necessary, think of the kid you had a crush on in grade school or something. She'll ask questions and sympathize about how hard it is to be away from the ones you love. You say something sweet about her and how kind she is. She starts babbling about whoever she's with. It'll be fine."

Both Jerry and Lena nodded their agreement as if Annie had perfectly planned out exactly how to handle the evening. Tommy bit his lip until Jerry frowned at him. Hopefully it would be that easy. Somehow he doubted that it would. His luck has never been that great for things like this. They all froze instinctively as one of the attendants appeared at the door.

"Showtime, kid," Jerry said, patting Tommy's shoulder. "Don't even try to hide the nervousness. Mistress Teolinda loves that."

"Thanks," Tommy said as he tried to swallow around the lump in his throat.

Hopefully this wouldn't be too bad. Tommy had a long ways to go before his father's gambling debt was paid off. He couldn't afford to screw it up on the very first night he got to work for real. The thought of a nice tip was enough to get

Tommy moving out into the hallway after the others even though he was nervous enough that he thought he could have thrown up, if only there was anything in his stomach.

2. SELECTION

Teolinda hummed as she followed the attendant to her chosen room. Hong's brothels were never her favorite place to play but she had the most delicious debt slaves working for her so Teolinda put up with it. The black paint made the hallway entirely too dark, especially when coupled with wall sconces that only lit about two square feet around them. If it weren't for the dim golden track lighting along the floor she would already have tripped and broken an ankle.

"This is your room, Mistress," the little attendant said with a perfectly respectful bow that made Teolinda smile at her. "I'll be back shortly with the available slaves."

"Thank you, dear," Teolinda said.

She slipped the girl a tip, nothing major but enough to earn a real smile out of the little thing. Inside, Teolinda's room was much better lit. The lights had been turned up, or perhaps turned on, so that everything was visible. Instead of black walls and carpet from the hallway, this room was decorated in shades of green and gold. The big bed with its heavy four-poster bed frame was decorated with both gorgeous green velvet drapes and every sort of cuff and tie-down one could ever want. The couch on the other side of the room was warm nubby brown velvet with luscious gold pillows that Teolinda immediately started planning uses for.

Better than the décor there was a rack that held a beautiful array of red silk corsets, silk dresses and more red silk scarfs than even Teolinda owned. She clapped her hands, only glancing at the buffet meal that Hong's people had set up. The cold cuts, bread and cheese were utterly average though it smelled as though the warming dish held hot wings. That was somewhat more promising. It would be decent, acceptable for snacking, but nothing to remember. The clothes were far more interesting as far as Teolinda was concerned.

It was a pity that Kim was so reluctant to let Teolinda dress hir up. Granted, Kim dealt with entirely too many people imposing their ideas of what proper apparel for hir would be but it still would be fun to do. A pair of tight jeans topped with a man's silk dress shirt cinched in by a luscious corset would be perfectly genderqueer, just like Kim. Add some nice spike heels and Kim would be stunning.

Of course, it wasn't going to happen but Teolinda did like thinking about it. Her visits to Hong's brothels were a chance to indulge her love for dressing other people up, among other kinks.

The scarves were wonderful, some long and thin, some small and square. A great number of them looked as though they'd been explicitly designed for tying someone up. That was a delight that made Teolinda grin. It was always so much fun to tie the slaves here up and then have her way with them. They were always so responsive, or at least they pretended very well.

Teolinda drifted away from the rack with its beautiful array of clothing, settling on the couch. Yes, she would have to dress whoever she chose up, possibly in one of the corsets or maybe in an array of scarves tied strategically around their body. And certainly she would have to tie them to the bed for play time. That was always fun.

"Mistress?" a voice called while knocking gently at the door.

"Come," Teolinda called.

She smiled as the attendant let the debt slaves in. Annie squealed when she saw Teolinda, running over to laugh as she snuggled in Teolinda's arms. That made Teolinda laugh, too. Playing with Annie was always full of laughter and sly gossip about the other Masters and Mistresses that Annie had played with recently. More than a couple times Teolinda had gotten a leg up on certain other Masters because of things that Annie let slip.

"Good to see you, Mistress," Jerry said as he came over more slowly. He might have pretended to be more dignified than Annie but he wasn't far behind her. He curled up next to her, pressing a kiss against Teolinda's cheek while poking at Annie to try and claim a hug from Teolinda.

"Good to see you too, Jerry," Teolinda laughed. "It's been entirely too long since I saw you. You must be getting close to paying off your debt."

"No, not yet," Jerry sighed, dramatically flopping his head on her shoulder only to obnoxiously peek down Teolinda's shirt. "Maybe soon?"

"Shameless boy," Teolinda snickered as she pushed him away only to have him sigh as if he was pining. "Utterly shameless boy!"

"He always has been." The deep Southern drawl made Teolinda gasp and pay attention to the other debt slaves available to her tonight.

"Lena!" Teolinda exclaimed, holding out her hands as Lena majestically stalked over in a stunning scarlet dress that was all but falling off her lean frame. "Come here and give me a kiss, you gorgeous girl, you!"

The kiss was everything that Teolinda liked, tongue and deep murmurs of pleasure mixed with hugs that pressed the two of them together. By the end of it Lena's dress had fallen down around her waist, much to Annie's amusement. It was only as Lena sighed dramatically, always dramatically, that Teolinda noticed the new boy hovering by the door.

"Oh goodness, you're adorable," Teolinda said, grinning at him.

"Um, thank you, Mistress," he said, pale cheeks going bright red as he ran his hands over his long, lean thighs. He couldn't be a day over twenty, if that.

Someone with some common sense had told him what to wear or he had excellent taste in clothes. His tank top was translucent red silk and the scarlet hot pants were tight enough to tell Teolinda exactly what the boy had to offer. They suited his coloring and his build, as did the nipple rings peeking through the top. Annie giggled, waving at him to come over.

"Don't worry, Tommy," Annie said. "Mistress Teolinda never bites. No guarantees on licking but no biting."

"Sorry," Tommy said as he hesitantly came over. "This is… well, new."

"You're his first customer," Lena said, chuckling at the way Tommy groaned. "He's terribly nervous about it all."

"Guys," Tommy complained.

He let Teolinda take his hand and didn't resist as she tugged him down to sit between him and Annie. As soon as he was sitting, Annie draped her arms around his neck, giggling at the way he squirmed. Teolinda grinned. The boy really was new to be squirming for this sort of thing. And he was adorable as he blushed and looked anywhere but Teolinda's very ample bust where it spilled out over her vest and silk shirt combination.

Hong was obviously angling to discover some particular information from Teolinda or she wouldn't have sent this particular group to Teolinda. Annie was always a tit for tat gossiper, given Teolinda as much information as she got. Jerry usually just admitted outright that he needed a particular bit of information so that he didn't have to fight and fuss and could just enjoy the sex. And Lena had been glorious fun to dress up as they gossiped together even though she'd been obviously uncomfortable with how large Teolinda was. Adding a new boy who was fresh out of training made it all the more obvious.

"Well, I don't mind you being nervous at all," Teolinda said. She smiled kindly at Tommy and then more widely when he gave her the most incredibly grateful look. "It's perfectly natural to be nervous your first time. Have you ever played with women?"

"Yeah," Tommy said hesitantly enough that Teolinda raised an eyebrow at him. "I mean, not like this. It was before I became a debt slave. All of this is new."

"But he did well in training," Jerry said in a sing-song voice that turned Tommy as red as his hot pants.

Teolinda laughed as she tugged Tommy into a hug. The boy all but melted into her arms, taking the hug as if he'd been dying to touch and was afraid of being punished for it. He made a little noise of contentment when Teolinda brushed a kiss against his hair that sounded utterly real. She grinned at Annie who giggled and wagged her eyebrows. Jerry was snickering behind a raised hand while Lena just angled her head at the door in an implicit question of whether they should leave Teolinda and Tommy alone.

Which meant that Tommy had been given explicit instructions to find something out; Teolinda sighed as she considered whether it was worth the inevitable awkward questioning to get to play with such a sweet, gentle boy. His sigh decided her. It had been a long time since she'd heard a grown man, which Tommy was despite his sweet nature and relative youth, sigh as if he was on the verge of tears for getting a little bit of love.

"You three go on," Teolinda said. "I think I'll take the honor of being Tommy's first."

"Have fun!" Annie sang as she bounced up off the couch, waving to Teolinda.

Lena looked utterly grateful as she stalked towards the door. In heels that high it wasn't as though she could do anything other than stalk. If she tried to hurry she'd probably break an ankle. Jerry grinned and stole a kiss before he left, shutting the door behind him so that Teolinda could be alone with Tommy.

"Mmm," Teolinda sighed as she cuddled Tommy despite the way he'd immediately stiffened. "I do love a good cuddle, sweetie. Really, don't fuss. Tonight will be fun and I've never been the sort to rape when my partner's not interested. If you don't like something just say so. We'll do something else."

Tommy frowned at her, pulling back just enough that she could see his face but not one inch farther. "But you must have something you want tonight, Mistress. Why else come here if you didn't?"

"Heh, what I want is to laugh and play dress up with someone who won't object to my fashion choices," Teolinda laughed, painfully aware that the laugh was just a bit too brittle, "and then maybe to have a little bit of mostly vanilla sex. I do like bondage but only with silk scarves. Other than that, I wanted a night out and some lovely clothes to play with."

"We're playing dress up dolls?" Tommy asked with so much disbelief that Teolinda burst out laughing. "Oh man, I'm sorry, Mistress! That was so rude."

"No," Teolinda said through her laughter. "No, it's okay! That's exactly right! Dress up and then playful sex just like little kids with dolls."

Tommy's disbelief melted into amusement and then a sort of willing acceptance that was incredibly rare in Teolinda's experience. He shrugged and settled in for another hug, chuckling quietly along with her only to sigh happily as she hugged him once more. From the way he responded, Tommy liked the feeling of Teolinda's ample body next to his and he was more than willing to let her dress him up in anything she chose.

"I think tonight is going to be a lot of fun," Teolinda said happily.

"Yeah," Tommy said, his smile shy and pleased. "I think it will, Mistress."

3. DRESS UP

Instead of immediately getting up, Mistress Teolinda held Tommy for about a half an hour. She dragged her nails over Tommy's back, the scratching exactly hard enough to make him groan and relax utterly in her arms. The others' advice seemed reasonable so Tommy didn't ask anything, didn't offer anything. It had been an incredibly long time since he'd been held. Tommy wished that every night could be like this until his debt was paid off.

"I think if you keep doing that I'm going to fall asleep," Tommy eventually sighed. "Regrettably."

"Well, we can't have that," Mistress Teolinda laughed. "Come on, up with you, sweet pea. I want to see what might look good on you. Did you choose the clothes or did someone else?"

"Oh, that was me," Tommy said as he sat up and then smiled as Mistress Teolinda offered him a hand up.

He didn't need it any more than she did but it was a dominance gesture so Tommy went with it. As he stood he was surprised by how much strength Mistress Teolinda had in her arm. She was pretty large, easily a size twenty-two if he was judging her hips right, but there seemed to be quite a lot of muscle under the fat that cushioned her body.

"You have a good eye," Mistress Teolinda said as she led him over to the rack of clothes. "The colors and styles you chose show your body off really well."

"Thank you, Mistress," Tommy said, far more pleased than he should be by the compliment.

"Do you like dresses?" Mistress Teolinda asked as she looked at several of the dresses on the rack.

Tommy blinked as his half-formed thoughts of tight pants and sexy shirts dissolved in the face of the possibility of spending the night crossdressing. He hadn't ever done it but Mistress Teolinda was the one paying so he had no real problem with it.

The problem was with the dress that she held out as an option. It was a silk shift dress with a dramatically plunging back and a beautiful swag of fabric draping across the chest. Unfortunately he could see from there that the skirt flared out dramatically, far too dramatically for someone who had no waist or hips at all to give it form.

"I don't think that one would work," Tommy said thoughtfully. "I don't have enough of a waist or hips for it. Bust would be fine with that drape but the rest of it would hang horribly on me. I mean, I don't mind dresses, Mistress, but probably not that one."

She grinned at him as if he'd just said the most wonderful thing ever. Mistress Teolinda hung the dress back up and then hugged him quickly before dragging him close so that they could go through the dresses together. He blushed at the approval but went willingly enough. This was a lot less terrifying than the beatings that Urith got or the way Vincent always came back from his nights with stitches and bandages all across his back and chest.

"I'm glad you don't mind them," Mistress Teolinda said.

"My lover Kim would be gorgeous in some of these but well, ze won't let me dress hir up."

Tommy blinked at her, surprised that he'd already gotten part of what he needed. "Your lover is genderqueer? Or trans*?"

"Genderqueer," Mistress Teolinda said with a little shrug. She peered at Tommy a little suspiciously. "Does that bother you?"

"No," Tommy said perfectly honestly. "I haven't seen many people like that since Mistress Hong bought my debt. She's um... well, she doesn't allow trans* or genderqueer people to work in the brothels."

That got him a disgusted snort from Mistress Teolinda. He could tell that she wasn't looking at the clothes on the rack anymore. All of her attention was on her anger at whatever memories he'd brought to mind. Still, Tommy didn't think it was a total loss. His mission was to find out about her lover and he seemed to be doing just fine so far. Genderqueer and first name of Kim was a good start.

"Oh, that one's nice," Tommy said.

"Hmm? Oh, the velvet one?" Mistress Teolinda said, snapping out of whatever memories had her scowling. "It is nice. I don't think it would suit you, though."

"No, trust me, it will, Mistress," Tommy said as he stripped the shirt off and then shucked off the too tight hot pants. He was a little embarrassed that his cock immediately responded by hardening after its release but Mistress Teolinda smiled at him so it was okay. "Let me try it on."

"Really?" Mistress Teolinda asked even as she took it off the hanger and unzipped the back.

Tommy nodded. He grinned as Mistress Teolinda helped slide the dress on. It was a little too snug at the waist but the dramatically draped dolman sleeves contrasted beautifully with that bit of snugness. Its skirt was tight enough that he wouldn't have been able to walk except that the right side was slit right up to the hip. When Tommy grinned and posed, one hip thrust out and a deliberately exaggerated pout on his lips Mistress Teolinda burst out laughing, applauding.

"It does look good!" Mistress Teolinda exclaimed. "I wouldn't have thought it."

"Makes up for my lack of hips very nicely," Tommy chuckled.

"We can fix that," Mistress Teolinda said as she pulled out a corset. "Have you worn one before?"

He stared at the one she'd picked. It was made of heavy red brocade with lush roses and fine green piping at the seams. The top was decorated with delicate lace that he was pretty sure was worth a significant percentage of his debt. The bottom had a lace flounce as wide as his hand. When Tommy gently touched it the corset felt like it was as rigid as steel. Away from the boning it was stiff, too, as if it had been lined with something so sturdy that nothing would make the fabric stretch or flex.

"No," Tommy said slowly. "I mean, they had us try on little waist nippers when I was in training but nothing like that. It's a lot more serious than the elastic things we wore."

Mistress Teolinda smiled, her eyes drooping shut in a look that was almost predatory if it weren't for how soft and kind she seemed. "I'd love to see you in it, Tommy. Actually, I'd like to put you in it, tie you up and gradually tighten it to see how much you can take."

Tommy licked his lips as he considered that. He'd been very nervous every time he'd been bound in training but it was different now with Mistress Teolinda. He was pretty sure that she'd let him stop the play if he got too uncomfortable and the hyperventilation that had made his previous experiences with bondage so unpleasant might be less if he was wearing the corset.

"Um, okay?" Tommy said, shivering as she grinned toothily at him. "I might freak out a little bit if I'm tied too tight. I'm not very well trained at that sort of thing."

"Oh, sweetie," Mistress Teolinda said as she pulled him in for a gentle little kiss. "I prefer silk scarf bondage. It's more a visual thing than a restraint thing. I'll probably loosely tie your ankles to your thighs and your wrists in front of you but that's about it. And then when we head to bed I'll probably tie you down but again it'll be easy to get out if you need to."

"I can handle that," Tommy whispered. "Thank you, Mistress. That helps a lot."

She grinned and kissed him again, much more passionately this time. Tommy leaned into the kiss, letting her hold him and pet him through the velvet dress. He wasn't at all surprised when the zipper slid down so that Mistress Teolinda could slide it off his shoulder. Rather than commenting, Tommy just stepped out of the dress and then held his arms up so that she could wrap the corset around him.

"Beautiful boy," Mistress Teolinda cooed. "Now, you give me a second to loosen the laces and I'll get this wrapped around that gorgeous body of yours."

"Yes, Mistress," Tommy said.

He grinned as she loosened the laces and then carefully had him hold the corset so that she could close it. The inside was lined with a lovely soft silk, reassuring Tommy somewhat. At least it wasn't lined with some harsh canvas that would leave marks on his body. Once the front busk was closed Mistress Teolinda moved around the back to tighten the laces back up again. Tommy bit his lip as it slowly constricted his ribcage and waist, surprised to find himself getting harder for this. It wasn't a kink he'd been aware of until now.

The corset was designed with a nip in at the waist, drawing his stomach ever inwards as Mistress Teolinda pulled the laces tighter and tighter. It was just short enough that his nipple piercings swung over the top edge instead of being caught inside. He deliberately raised his chest, breathing in and letting it out slowly as the trainers had told him was best when getting laced into a corset. That helped keep his rib cage from feeling as though it was going to be crushed, not that he thought that would actually happen. Mistress Teolinda didn't seem the sort for causing injury.

"Just snug," Mistress Teolinda said, patting Tommy's bare bottom. "How's it feel?"

"Tight," Tommy said, wiggling a little and then smiling because it was a good bit more flexible than he'd thought it would be. "Not as tight as I thought it would be."

Mistress Teolinda laughed, wrapping her arms around Tommy so that she could nuzzle his ear while gently stroking his cock. It hardened dramatically at her touch, enough so that Tommy blushed and squirmed a little. He couldn't squirm as much as normal with the corset around his torso.

"We're only just starting on the tightening, Tommy," Mistress Teolinda said. "Come on, let's go cuddle on the couch while you get used to this. It'll take three or four rounds before I'm ready to tie you up and then see just how much you can take."

Tommy groaned, letting her lead him over to the couch by his cock. Tonight was going to be really interesting in so many ways. Hopefully he'd manage to remember his mission. With how aroused she'd gotten him already Tommy wasn't sure just how coherent he was going to be or for how long.

4. PLAY TIME

"It's so tight."

Teolinda smiled at Tommy's red cheeks, the way he shifted his feet and tried to get more comfortable. It had taken nearly an hour and a half of off and on tightening to get to this point. Tommy's waist was inches narrower, giving him a visible hourglass when he normally had no such thing. The wonderful part was how he had responded to her tightening the corset.

Instead of groaning or complaining as some of the other debt slaves did, Tommy had only whimpered with arousal and whined when she stopped. When Teolinda had suggested stopping, Tommy had shaken his head no, staring over his shoulder with such an obvious plea for more that she'd gone ahead and tightened the corset another quarter inch and then another. It was so tight now that the back was nearly completely shut at the waist, though of course there was still room at the rib cage and hips.

He'd protested being made to kneel until Teolinda had kissed him and waggled a silk scarf in front of his face. Then he'd knelt so willingly that she had thought about stripping and letting him fuck her out right then and there. But it had been too soon for that with his corset not fully tightened and not one scarf restraining him. Now would be perfect but she wanted to enjoy his body a little bit more first.

"You look lovely," Teolinda murmured as she ran her hands down his rib cage and over his unnaturally slender waist. "Most men don't take to corsets so well. Well, few women do either, more's the pity."

Each of Tommy's breaths was short and sharp, appropriate to both the constriction around his torso as well as how hard his exposed cock was. It wept, slowly dripping on the carpet between his spread knees. His ankles were bound to his thighs with red silk scarves, just as his wrists were in front of him with another scarlet piece of silk. She smiled as she bent once more to run her hands over his shoulders, trailing her fingers down to the ruby drops suspended from his nipple piercings. The smell of his arousal filled the air, driving out even the smell of the hot wings on the buffet table.

"Do you like it?" Teolinda asked. She tugged the piercings, smiling at his gasp and moan. "Or is it too much?"

"No," Tommy panted. "No, Mistress. It's, it's good. Very good. Just… it's so tight!"

He whined, so obviously turned on by the feeling of being restrained and adorned by the corset that Teolinda couldn't help but lick her lips. He truly was a stunningly attractive young man. His slim limbs and wide brown eyes would be more than enough to tempt her even if it weren't for the gloss still shimmering on his lips and his hips thrusting desperately at the air.

"Mmm, I'm glad that you like it then," Teolinda murmured as her own arousal rose to the point that she couldn't push it down anymore. "If I untie your legs do you think you can walk to the bed for me? I think I'd like to ride you this way,

Tommy, with your hands tied over your head and the corset making you so very beautiful."

"Please, Mistress!"

Tommy's cheeks went even redder as he flushed down to the top of the corset. He licked the gloss on his lips and nodded urgently. Teolinda chuckled as she knelt to loosen the knots binding his legs. Really, the boy was a treasure. She'd have to see if she could get Tommy again the next time she visited this brothel. The boy was tempting enough that she might even consider the trade deal Hong asked about last week if time with Tommy was put into the contract.

"There you go," Teolinda said as the last knot binding his legs slipped free. She left his hands tied for the moment, though she did give him a hand up. The sweet boy was shaking already. "Up you get. I'm looking forward to seeing just how much you're enjoying this."

"Oh God, please ride my face a little bit too, Mistress," Tommy begged as he struggled to his feet and then walked on wobbly legs to the big, comfortable bed. "Please! I want, I want so much, so much, you're beautiful and oh God, it's...!"

He whined as he sat on the edge of the bed, eyes so desperate that Teolinda's breath caught nearly as badly as his. Oh yes, she was going to enjoy her time with Tommy to the maximum and she was going to make use of him every chance she got. She freed his hands only to retie them to the center O-ring on the headboard. The scarf was looped fairly loosely. He should be able to slip free if he needed to. He groaned as she ran her hands down his body, over the nipple rings and corset, all the way to his cock where it stuck proudly up into the air.

"Mistress..." Tommy whispered, jerking at the touch so badly that she would have thought that he'd been hit by an electric shock.

"Don't worry, Tommy," Teolinda purred as she took one

of the condoms from the basket on the bedside table. "You'll get everything you want and so much more. I have plans for tonight's play that I think we'll both enjoy."

She rolled the condom onto his cock before stripping her clothes off. It was always a nervous moment for Teolinda. So many people reacted poorly to the swell of her belly, the sag of her breasts. Even the best trained debt slaves tended to flinch for a moment when they first saw her naked. Teolinda wasn't upset with her body and had never seen the need to diet to match what society called 'beautiful'. Being strong and fit was more important and the extra inches had never kept her from doing what she wanted to.

Still, it hurt when a sexual partner flinched on seeing her body for the first time. To Teolinda's delight, Tommy didn't flinch at all. His eyes went wide, the eyes dilating a little bit, while his cock jerked against his belly. His groan of appreciation was so heartfelt that Teolinda giggled as she climbed on the bed with you.

"Beautiful boy," Teolinda crooned as she guided his cock in. "Tell me if it's too much. You're not going to be able to breathe normally with the corset."

"I know," Tommy panted, moaned, panted some more. "I know! I like it. Oh God, Mistress, it feels so good!"

His panting turned into stunned silence as Teolinda started to move. She set her hands on either side of his head and rode Tommy as though he was a stallion. The harder she moved the more he seemed to like it, letting Teolinda drive for one orgasm, and then with a slight shift of angle that let his cock hit different spots inside, a second and then finally a third that made her throw her head back and shout.

"Mistress!" Tommy shouted as she clamped down on him, biting his lip and holding his breath until she tapped his stomach to make him stop. "Oh God, oh God, so good! Please, please more, please!"

"Do you think you can set your feet and thrust up into me?" Teolinda asked with a breathless laugh that would make Kim grin at her.

"Please!" Tommy begged.

She shifted around and then gasped as Tommy did exactly that. They were good hard trusts, short and fast but that was good. That was perfect, especially as Tommy's face took on a look of intense concentration and his arms began to tremble. Teolinda shuddered as she shifted angle just enough to let him hammer right against her G-spot. Pretty soon she was shaking harder than he was.

"Don't stop," Teolinda ordered, the words broken and breathless. "Don't stop! Don't stop, don't stop, don't stop… Oh yes!"

This time when Teolinda came it was one of the really big orgasms that made her head spin and her whole body lock up. She heard Tommy scream as he bucked up into her only to freeze as he came. She barely managed to get her arms underneath her before she flopped on top of Tommy. To her surprise Tommy was completely limp other than his still hard cock.

"Oh dear," Teolinda laughed quietly. "Poor baby passed out."

It only took a couple of moments to slide off and remove the condom. By that point Tommy was already waking back up. He blinked at Teolinda with such a confused expression that she petted his cheek before untying his hands. More bondage could obviously wait. The sweet boy had gone so deep into subspace that he was all but limp as she rolled him over to start loosening the corset.

Removing it was much faster than putting it on had been. Teolinda did her best to loosen the laces evenly but she didn't fuss too much about it. It wasn't her personal corset, after all, so it hardly mattered. Hong's people would straighten it out later on, after Teolinda had gone home. Which wasn't going to be for a little while; Tommy was too adorable not to cuddle and maybe have a second round with.

"Come here, sweet pea," Teolinda said once Tommy was free. "Time for a cuddle."

"Mmm-hmm," Tommy murmured as he let her wrap him up in her arms.

His expression was even more content than before, happy, sated and utterly grateful all at once. And once again, there was no sign that he had any issues at all with Teolinda's size. She smiled as she gently scratched his back. The next time she came back to the brothel she would have to specifically request Tommy. He was exactly what Teolinda looked for when she visited.

"Thank you, Mistress," Tommy mumbled against the swell of her breast.

"Heh, you're welcome, Tommy," Teolinda replied. "You don't get much cuddling, do you?"

5. STORY TIME

The question came through the haze of pleasure slowly at first. It took Tommy a few moments to remember that this wasn't just two people playing together. He had a mission and this might be the perfect opening to get Mistress Teolinda to start talking. She didn't seem to be in any rush to hear his answer but he shouldn't wait too long.

"No, never did," Tommy admitted. "My mom died when I was really young and my dad was a gambler. He was more likely to hit than to hug even when he did win."

"Oh, baby," Mistress Teolinda sighed, squeezing him in a firmer hug than he would have expected. "You were taken away?"

"No, no," Tommy laughed. He pulled back just enough to be able to meet her eyes. It really was nice getting cuddled this way. "I just spent a lot of time with friends, couch surfing, visiting. Stuff like that. It was never really bad. Most of the time he just... spent too much on his gambling. He's in a treatment program now. I took on his debt so that he could go and get over his addiction. There just wasn't much... cuddling."

His shrug and blatant attempt to snuggle between her breasts made Mistress Teolinda laugh. She not only encouraged him, she pulled him in to press butterfly kisses all over his face. That got him laughing too, which made Mistress Teolinda laugh harder. In just a minute they dissolved into giggles in each other's arms.

"You really took your father's debt?" Mistress Teolinda asked they'd gotten their breath back.

"Yeah," Tommy said. "He wasn't the best dad in the world but he wasn't horrible. I mean, some of the others have horror stories like you wouldn't believe about their families. My dad wasn't bad. He would go gamble every so often and once he started he couldn't stop, even if he'd lost his limit. Then he'd swear to stay away from the casinos, pay down his gambling debt and eventually go back. It just got to the point where he wouldn't pay it down enough and the debt built and well, here I am. Give it three or six months and he'll probably be out of the treatment program."

Mistress Teolinda frowned, running her fingers over Tommy's cheek as if worried about him. "And then what? Will he take his debt back? Or are you stuck paying it off?"

"According to the agreement we both signed, he gets treatment and then takes my place in the debt slavery program," Tommy said. "Whatever I earn gets taken off the debt but the rest is all his. It'll work out."

Her body was warm enough that there was a faint sheen of sweat between them. Fortunately, the rest of the room was warm enough that Tommy felt no need to crawl under the covers. It would have been much too warm if they had. Honestly, he wasn't sure if they were even supposed to get under the covers. The way the bed had been made didn't make doing so easy.

He dismissed the wild thoughts as Mistress Teolinda's frown faded into an expression that looked sadder, lonelier.

Tommy automatically hugged her to try and make her feel better. Keeping the customers happy was definitely part of his job. He'd taken more than one beating for not answering correctly on questions about that.

"I'm fine, sweetie," Mistress Teolinda murmured.

"You look sad, Mistress," Tommy replied. "I'm sorry I made you sad."

"Oh, it wasn't you." Mistress Teolinda chuckled and then sighed. "Wasn't you at all, sweet boy."

"Then what's wrong?" Tommy asked. He let his face do whatever it wanted. It felt like the puppy eyes that Annie had talked about and Mistress Teolinda beamed at him so he'd probably managed a good, encouraging expression.

She kissed him, pulling him up for a snuggle that turned amorous as his idiot cock decided that he should rub against her belly and thighs. Mistress Teolinda grinned and gripped his hips, encouraging him so Tommy went with it. Pretty quickly she pushed him onto his back so that she could roll another condom down his cock.

This round was a lot better, or at least Tommy was able to focus on it better. It was pretty obvious that Mistress Teolinda preferred riding over being ridden because she very firmly kept him on his back as she ground down onto his erection. Of course, she did bend over, dropping her beautiful breasts into his face so Tommy started sucking on her nipples and playing with them.

"Oh yes!" Mistress Teolinda gasped. "That! Do that! Harder!"

He flicked his tongue over her nipple, rocking his hips to add to the sensations for both of them. It didn't take long before Mistress Teolinda gasped and came, clamping down hard enough on him that he winced. She didn't slow down, barely even paused, as she fucked herself on him. It took almost half an hour before Tommy was on the verge of another orgasm and in that time he lost track of how many orgasms Mistress Teolinda had.

"Can't... Can't hold, Mistress," Tommy gasped.

"Good, good, hard," Mistress Teolinda panted. "Fuck me hard!"

Tommy planted his feet and thrust up into her as hard as he could. At the same time he pinched her nipples and pulled on them, stretching her breasts out until she screamed her way through a massive orgasm that pulled Tommy over the edge, too. He shouted and then grunted when Mistress Teolinda collapsed on top of him. She was heavy but not heavy enough that he wanted her to move, especially not given the spasms that kept squeezing his cock.

"Oh God," Tommy groaned. "You really gotta come back, Mistress."

Mistress Teolinda giggled, pressing a wet kiss against Tommy's neck. Eventually she rolled off and let Tommy take care of the condom. As soon as that was done she pulled Tommy back into her arms for more cuddling that made him sigh happily. He wasn't sure if he should ask anything else but after a couple of minutes of very comfortable, if slightly giggly, snuggle time Mistress Teolinda sighed.

"It wasn't you," Mistress Teolinda murmured. "My Kim's parents were a lot like yours except hir mother was the gambler and hir father was an alcoholic. There was... a lot of abuse."

"Huh, well if ze's genderqueer then I'm not surprised by that," Tommy huffed. "Not to be rude but some older people are really reactionary about people who don't fit 'male' or 'female'. Bugs me. They're not hurting anyone. Ought to just leave them alone and let them live their lives."

The hug this time was almost smothering but Tommy went with it. He could feel Mistress Teolinda shivering slightly as if that was exactly what she'd needed to hear when she needed to hear it. Once she let go he got a serious, long, passionate kiss that normally would have convinced his penis to sit up and pay attention. Two orgasms so quickly made that impossible, though.

"You are too sweet to be real," Mistress Teolinda said.

Her almost suspicious look made Tommy snort as he put on the most exaggeratedly innocent expression he could manage. "Why Mistress, I have no idea what you're talking about!"

"Oh God," Mistress Teolinda laughed, her belly and breasts shaking from her mirth. "That's horrible!"

He kept making faces at her until there were tears in her eyes and she was hiccupping as much as laughing. Then several minutes of kissing and making out were needed before the hiccups died down. She grinned at him, the suspicion far enough gone that he could relax again. When she started running her nails through Tommy's hair he groaned dramatically.

"Don't stop," Tommy sighed.

"You should have been born a cat," Mistress Teolinda snickered. "I have to bring Kim here to meet you. We'd have so much fun playing with you, sweet boy."

"Mistress," Tommy said, letting his face show every bit of the contentment he felt at this moment, "I'd be happy to be yours anytime you come in. For anything you might want to do."

She grinned and wagged her eyebrows. "How about we put you in one of the waist nippers and see how many of the dresses fit?"

Tommy leaned in and kissed her, taking it slow and gentle. At first Mistress Teolinda giggled but within seconds her hands were on either side of Tommy's face, holding him in place as she deepened the kiss into something that made him shiver with appreciation and hopeless lust. They both needed to drink something as their mouths had gone sour but Tommy didn't care.

All that really mattered was kissing Mistress Teolinda and caressing her body until she moaned into his mouth. Hopefully she'd want to keep him for several more hours, maybe all night. That would be wonderful. And if he could convince her to come back with her lover Kim then he'd have fulfilled his mission in spades. Tommy was sure that Mistress Hong would be able to learn all sorts of things if they were both here playing with Tommy.

Eventually Mistress Teolinda let Tommy's lips go, smiling at him. He smiled back and pressed a kiss on the tip of her nose. She giggled before pushing him away with an expression that looked nearly as happy as Tommy felt.

"I'd like to have you dress me up, Mistress," Tommy said. "I'd like to get to eat you until my tongue feels like it's going to fall off. I'd like to cuddle and fall asleep in your arms. I think I'd like pretty much anything we did together so what do you want to do?"

"Let's get up, nibble on those wings," Mistress Teolinda said as she sat up and took Tommy's hand, "and then see just how many of those outfits will work for you."

"Sounds great, Mistress!" Tommy said.

He wasn't surprised that he meant every word. Tonight was a far better night than he'd expected and as long as they were together there were more chances to learn what Mistress Hong wanted to know. Tommy let Mistress Hong help him up and then held her hand as they went to check out the buffet.

Yeah, tonight wasn't too bad. Hopefully the rest of his career as a debt slave would be similarly straightforward. Even as he thought it Tommy knew that it was ridiculously wishful thinking. All he had to do was look at the other debt slaves to know that tonight was probably going to be one of the nights he remembered while trying to survive the other Masters he'd play with.

Mistress Teolinda's easy smile helped Tommy push the bad thoughts away. There would be time enough later, when he reported in on what he'd learned, to ponder just how fucked up his life had become. For now he had a sweet, wonderful Mistress to pamper and play with. Living for the moment wasn't something he normally did but right now it seemed like the best idea ever.

6. STOCKINGS

"Now those are nice," Teolinda said as Tommy adjusted the garter holding his scarlet silk stockings up. "I wish they had some heels in your size tonight."

"I don't, Mistress," Tommy laughed. "I'm always afraid I'm going to break my ankle when I wear heels. I mean, I learned how in training but I never feel stable on them."

"That's part of the point!" Teolinda laughed at his disgusted expression before handing him a pair of women's panties to put on.

Tommy shook his head as he slid the panties on. It took some serious tucking to get the panties to settle in properly but eventually he looked wonderfully female. They'd found a nice little waist nipper that was more elastic than boning. It drew his waist in without the same degree of discomfort and bruising that the corset had caused.

Teolinda was fairly certain that Tommy didn't realize that he had some bruises forming from the boning along his back. She'd been concerned that the previous corset had been too tight but Tommy's enthusiasm for the process of tightening had reassured her. Next time she'd remember that Tommy's pain threshold was a little too high for tight lacing play.

"I think a nice bra would help the look," Teolinda mused as she walked around Tommy, running her hands over his body. "Maybe that push-up bra that matches the stockings."

"We do that and my cock isn't going to stay tucked very well, Mistress," Tommy said. He shivered for the touches even as he grinned over his shoulder at Teolinda.

"That's incentive!" Teolinda said, grinning as he laughed.

The push-up bra added just the right touch to Tommy's latest outfit. Even with his short hair and obviously masculine features, he looked delightfully female. Teolinda licked her lips as she stared at him, eyes sweeping him from head to toes. She wasn't surprised as Tommy shifted position nervously at her predatory expression.

He blushed when the change of position let his cock slip free from between his legs. Teolinda grinned as Tommy tried to tuck it back in even though he was slowly hardening. She caught his wrist and pulled his hands away. When she gently pushed his hands behind his back Tommy moaned.

"I think I want to play with that some more," Teolinda murmured as she took one of the long thin silk scarves. "Hands behind your back."

"Yes, Mistress," Tommy said.

He put his hands exactly in the right position behind his back, wrists crossed and palms facing outwards. Tommy's fingertips trembled slightly but then his breath was so fast that Teolinda wasn't worried. She secured his wrists with the scarf, making sure that the knot wouldn't slide and cut off circulation if Tommy struggled. Heavy bondage had never been Teolinda's thing. She just liked the way subs behaved when they didn't have freedom of movement.

When Teolinda moved back around to stand in front of Tommy his cock was fully hard. Better than that, he was leaving a lovely damp spot on the panties. She grinned and stroked him through the panties. Tommy gasped, eyes going wide and then falling shut as he moaned.

The silk panties felt lovely to Teolinda. She was sure that they felt even more wonderful to Tommy's cock. His hips jerked at every movement of Teolinda's hands. As she stroked him the damp spot got even bigger, making the panties stick instead of slide smoothly.

"Tisk," Teolinda whispered as she rubbed the wet spot down the length of his cock. "You're getting them all dirty, Tommy."

"Sorry, Mistress," Tommy apologized.

"Will you make it up to me?" Teolinda asked as she adjusted his cock in the panties. When she was done the tip stuck up past the waistband's lacy elastic, letting his cock weep as much as it wanted.

"Yes, Mistress!" Tommy nodded, licking his lips hopefully.

Teolinda chuckled even though she was surprised at his continued interest in eating her out. It was rare for her to encounter someone who truly wanted that. Kim loved oral sex. Most of the time that was what they did in bed together. She hadn't given any serious thought to allowing Tommy to do it as well.

"Mmm, well, I might allow that," Teolinda said and then paused because Tommy's eyes dilated at the hint of being allowed oral sex. "But you have to be good for me."

"Please, Mistress!" Tommy begged.

He didn't jerk his arms but he did flex his shoulders and whimper as if she was torturing him. Teolinda shivered and nodded. Her plans for the rest of the evening obviously had to be adjusted. Even if she didn't let him eat her out, she could ride him again and enjoy his wonderful cock. She held up a hand for Tommy to stay where he was as she went back to the clothing rack.

None of the dresses were perfect for the image she had in her mind. If there had been a georgette dress with a froth of lace at the hem that would have been ideal. She wanted something translucent that allowed her to see Tommy's body and the lingerie that they'd chosen so far but she also wanted something that flowed and that took a bit more substance that the little lace teddies and nightgowns had.

"Oh, now that's an idea," Teolinda commented as she pulled a pair of burgundy harem pants from the rack. "Just the right level of translucency too!"

There was a matching cropped top, an absurdly short mock tunic that had delicately embroidered leaves along the neckline, hem and cuffs. Teolinda nodded as she pulled both of them off their hangers. Normally Teolinda didn't like mixing masculine garments with feminine underthings but in this case it worked perfectly.

Tommy didn't move at all as Teolinda freed his wrists from the scarf. She draped it around her neck for the moment and then helped him into the harem pants. They sat low enough on his hips that the very tip of his cock peeked out, wet and dripping in ways that made Teolinda think very hard about enormous tips.

The tunic was exquisite when Teolinda had Tommy slip into it. It draped around his chest, hanging off the bra as if he actually had breasts instead of a well-engineered undergarment. The best part was that it left his waist free so that she could see the waist nipper and his cock.

After a moment's consideration of the picture Tommy presented, Teolinda shook her head and removed the waist nipper while leaving the garter and stockings in place. Their arch across his hips contrasted beautifully with the harem pants' waistband. Underneath, she could see the stockings and panties.

"The only sad part is that the bra hides your adorable

pierced nipples," Teolinda said as she moved back behind Tommy. "Ah well, you can't have everything. I'll have to ask for some shelf bras next time. Then I could have it all."

Tommy moaned something so incoherent that Teolinda wasn't sure if he'd intended to say 'yes please', 'oh fuck', or just 'Mistress'.

Once again, when Teolinda gestured for Tommy to stay where he was, he didn't move a muscle. His eyes followed her as she walked over to the couch to sit and stare up at him. Her leftover water was there, as was a little plate with three chicken wings. Teolinda slowly ate them, licking her fingers in such an exaggerated way that she wanted to giggle at herself.

Tommy didn't laugh. He swallowed so hard that it had to hurt his throat. The look he gave her was pure lust and need coupled with the sort of desperation that made Teolinda's breath catch. She licked her lips clean and then drank a bit more of the water. Maybe she would let him eat her. He looked so very desperate for it.

"Turn," Teolinda ordered, swirling one finger in a circle.

"Yes, Mistress," Tommy whispered, his voice husky and pained.

He slowly turned in place, letting her see the outfit on him. It really was a lovely effect and delightfully gender neutral. From the back he looked entirely female but then when he turned back to the side his cock was pressing against the underwear and harem pants' waistbands hard enough that they gaped away from his hips. A line of moisture had dribbled down his cock to soak into the waistband of the pants, darkening it too.

"Come here, sweet boy," Teolinda ordered. "I want you on your knees between my legs. Don't tear any of the clothes though."

"No, Mistress," Tommy said as he came over.

He moved gracefully despite how fiercely erect his cock was. To her surprise he managed to kneel without problems even with his hands bound behind his back. She smiled at him, caressing his cheeks and then finding the nipple rings under the bra to give them a firm tweak. Tommy jerked and gasped, cheeks going nearly as red as the lingerie on his body.

"I don't normally allow this," Teolinda told Tommy. She ran one finger over his bottom lip, smiling shyly. "Kim's the only one who's had it for quite a while."

"Really, Mistress?" Tommy asked, surprised enough that the haze of lust faded for a moment.

"Mm-hmm," Teolinda murmured. She grinned, feeling how hard and dangerous the smile was. "So you better be very good indeed, Tommy. I want your best."

The alert expression immediately disappeared under another wave of lust that made Tommy garble 'yes, Mistress' while groaning loudly. Teolinda leaned back on the couch, spreading her legs for Tommy. She couldn't stop her legs from shaking slightly. Nor could she stop her breath from speeding up. It was so incredibly intimate to allow this, far more so than riding a cock or dildo.

"Be good, Tommy," Teolinda ordered. "Make me happy."

7. REWARD

"Yes, Mistress," Tommy said.

Or at least tried to say. The words tangled on his tongue and turned into a garbled moan that didn't make sense even to him. He couldn't help but shake at getting this honor. It was an honor, a huge one. Tommy had been told so many times in training that the Masters and Mistresses that chose to play with him wouldn't give him anything personal. That wasn't what he was for and it wasn't something he should expect.

Tommy knew that years before he entered the debt slavery system. He'd known that before his mother died, frankly. People giving you a part of their heart and soul was incredibly rare. It had to be treated as a precious gift. All his life he'd done his best to be respectful and grateful when people opened up to him. This was no different from any other moment even if Mistress Teolinda was paying for his time and his body.

He bent carefully, mouthing his way up Mistress Teolinda's inner thigh. She smelled of the cherry lube they'd used last and buffalo wings overlaying the salty musk smell of a woman who'd come hard and promised to come even more. His silk clothing shifted around his body. The scarf around his wrists tightened until Tommy adjusted his arms a bit.

Mistress Teolinda's hands settled on the top of Tommy's head. She didn't grip his hair, sadly, but she also didn't push him away. Instead she only let her hands rest there as if she needed the contact to be able to handle him between her legs this way.

That made sense. It made a great deal of sense, enough sense that the haze of lust receded far enough to allow him to think again. He still didn't have Kim's last name but he did have the possibility of Mistress Teolinda returning with Kim. Tommy needed more and hopefully if he gave Mistress Teolinda the sort of orgasms she wanted he'd get more in the afterglow. At the very least he'd get to eat her out and that made the evening well worth it.

"Mmm," Tommy hummed as he finally kissed his way to her crotch.

Her hair had been trimmed short enough to be a bit spikey against his lips but not so sort as to give stubble burn. Tommy sighed over that, nuzzling her clit and rubbing his face against her groin as if it was the best thing ever. It sort of was. He couldn't remember the last time he'd had someone really willing to do this with. Training wasn't at all the same thing even if Tommy had been very good at it, good enough to give his partners real orgasms when they were supposed to be learning how to fake them.

The little noise made Mistress Teolinda's breath catch. His rubbing made her laugh and pet his hair. When he delicately tongued her clit she gasped and bucked as if shocked by the contact. Given how much sex they'd already had, Mistress Teolinda had to be sensitive already. Tommy grinned as he tongued her clit again.

"Fuck!" Mistress Teolinda grunted. She shifted so that she

was lying further back on the couch, her hips closer to Tommy's face. "More of that!"

"Yes, Mistress," Tommy said directly against her clit.

He deliberately used lots of tongue and lip as he said the words, letting his breath gust over her flesh. Goosebumps formed, followed by a full body shudder that made Tommy grin. Oh yeah, this was going to be wonderfully fun.

"Oh my God," Mistress Teolinda gasped as Tommy sucked her clit into his mouth.

The cherry lube was almost too strongly flavored in Tommy's opinion. It hid her taste until he let his tongue slide lower, down to her lips where he licked and sucked. Tommy did that for a few seconds before moving back up to mouth as much of her clit as he could. Mistress Teolinda was heavy enough that her clit hid inside her mound but he wiggled his head and pushed in with his lips and chin. The grunt he got from Mistress Teolinda turned into a groan and then panting gasps as he sucked rhythmically on her clit.

He was pretty sure that she wouldn't be able to handle too much of this. They'd fucked too much already for it to be an option for long. Tommy used his tongue against the tip of her clit while sucking reasonably hard. It was obvious when he found exactly the right pressure and speed because Mistress Teolinda's hands tightened on his hair, holding him exactly where he was.

"That, that, fuck, yes, that, that!" Mistress Teolinda panted.

She started rocking against his face, her hands holding him still in just the right ways to make Tommy's brain drain out his ears again. It felt so good to be held still and used this way, to bring her pleasure after she'd made Tommy feel so wonderful. The salty-musk smell increased as Mistress Teolinda's grunts turned into a wail. Her arms and legs locked tight, holding Tommy's face crushed against her clit.

Wetness flooded his chin but he couldn't move down to lick it away because Mistress Teolinda held on and rocked harder. Tommy groaned even though his air was limited. He sucked harder and faster, trying to give Mistress Teolinda another orgasm this way. She screamed at the increased pleasure, bucking so hard that Tommy almost felt like he'd been punched in the jaw.

Fortunately she also let go of his hair, letting Tommy get a gulp of air before he moved down to slide his tongue along the length of her pussy. Mistress Teolinda shuddered and pushed him away. Her laugh was as wobbly as her legs seemed to be when he pouted about it.

"Oh baby boy, I should have known you'd be good at that," Mistress Teolinda sighed.

"More, Mistress?" Tommy asked hopefully even though he could see that she was pretty much wiped out at last.

"No, no more," Mistress Teolinda chuckled. "Well, one more thing. I want you to rub that perfect little cock between by breasts until you come but then we're done for the night. Goodness, I don't know if my legs will hold me up long enough to go home."

She let Tommy's hands free which made it much easier to do as she wanted. To Tommy's surprise Mistress Teolinda sucked on his cock as well as letting him tit fuck her. It took long enough for Tommy to come that his legs and back ached but Mistress Teolinda didn't look as though she minded.

If anything, she hugged him all the harder once he was done. Tommy sort of expected that she would want him to help clean her up and help her dress but she planted a hand in the middle of Tommy's chest when he moved to try. Her smile was ruefully amused.

"Sweet boy, I'm so sensitive right now that I think my skin's trying to come off," Mistress Teolinda said.

"Sorry, Mistress," Tommy laughed. "I think my cock agrees with your skin."

She giggled and kissed Tommy, waving for him to pose in his sweat and come soaked harem pants and lingerie. It only took her about two minutes to get dressed again but she didn't put her personal corset back on. That got wrapped up and put into a big bag that Tommy hadn't noticed by the door.

"You were wonderful, Tommy," Mistress Teolinda said. "I think I'll request you personally when I come back."

"I'd love it if you did, Mistress," Tommy said. He shrugged and smiled as shyly as he could while staring straight at her breasts. "And um, if you want to bring Kim along I'd be glad to pay with hir as well."

"You are so sweet," Mistress Teolinda crooned. "Sleep well, Tommy."

"Good luck getting home, Mistress," Tommy said.

He waved as she left, holding the smile for several seconds after her departure just on the off chance she forgot something and came back in. The door stayed shut so Tommy sighed and relaxed a little. He stripped out of the clothes, nodding when the attendants came back in. They looked at him as if afraid that he'd be bloody and shaking with pain but Tommy shrugged.

"You'll want to get the sofa and rug as well as the bed," Tommy said. "We were all over the room."

"Yes, sir," the taller of the two attendants, both plain, both shy, both nervous, said. "Debrief is in Room C downstairs."

"Got it," Tommy replied.

He passed over the lingerie, rubbing his back and frowning as he realized that there were bruises forming back there. Tommy slipped out of the play room and then down the hallway to the back staircase they were supposed to use. As soon as the door shut behind him all the luxury and beauty of the brothel disappeared. The walls were drab gray that used to be white. The floor was stained linoleum. As he went down the stairs to the basement, the steps were bare concrete that no one had swept for months, at best.

Room C was as bleak as the dressing room or the back hallways, a simple square room with no windows. A steel table sat in the middle of the room. The attendant sitting at the table had obviously been chain smoking for a while because the room stank of cigarette smoke and sweat. He gestured at Tommy to take the hard plastic chair opposite him as he switched on a little recorder sitting by his nearly-full ashtray.

"Teolinda Horne, served by Tommy Leigh," the attendant said in an utterly bored tone of voice. "Speak slowly and clearly. Start with a recounting of events. Tell me everything that you learned that might be useful to Mistress Hong."

"Yes, sir," Tommy said, squirming a little on the chair.

The pleasure and love from the play room was already fading. Tommy bit his lip as he marshaled his thoughts. Looked at objective, he really hadn't learned all that much.

A first name and an identity as genderqueer wouldn't count as success to Mistress Hong. If he wanted to get out of this with his presumed tip intact he'd have to sell this as a building encounter rather than a fact-finding one. He nodded once, meeting the attendant's bored eyes.

"Um, well, this was my first client," Tommy said, watching the attendant's eyes glaze over in dull apathy. "It went... well, I guess?"

He started detailing everything that had happened as he'd been trained, always making a point to note the bits of information he'd found out about Kim's identity and personality. Tommy hoped that it would be enough. It had to be, honestly. There wasn't much that he could do now that Mistress Teolinda was gone home to improve his situation.

If he got really lucky the details he provided would be enough to pinpoint Kim's identity. And if life was treating Tommy well then Mistress Teolinda actually would come back to play again. He hoped that she would. Tonight had been wonderful enough that Tommy almost allowed himself to believe that working in a brothel wouldn't be an unmitigated nightmare.

Now if only the cynical part of his soul that had grown up with a gambler as a father wasn't busily calculating the odds of it happening. Tommy didn't need a reminder that his luck had always been terrible where people acting kindly were concerned.

As he finished his report, Tommy swallowed down the urge to pray that this wouldn't be the last bit of kindness he got for years to come.

He really didn't know if he could handle that.

The End

AUTHOR'S NOTE: THREE SISTERS

Tommy is one of my favorite characters. His story is one that will take quite a while to tell. I've got a full book planned for how he finally finds the love of his life. But these stories are much earlier in Tommy's life. After Teolinda, his clients aren't quite as wonderful, sadly.

1. DENIM

Raina smiled as Tommy's nails scrabbled over her thighs, the nails catching on the seams of her jeans. The denim protected her from his desperation, just as the blindfold over his eyes kept him from knowing what she was going to do next. It was a pity to take the boy's sight away from him. He was lovely when his dark brown eyes went wide at the feeling of her favorite vibrator pulsing away against his prostate.

Today's play required surprise though. Raina caressed his cheek, chuckling at his startled gasp. His tongue darted out to touch his top lip before retreating again, leaving a shining wet spot behind. Raina didn't allow herself to shiver as she watched it flit into view and then away.

Instead she bent and kissed him, licking his bottom lip to coax his tongue back out again. Tommy whined, his face hot in her hands. She held him still for the kiss that followed. His hips pulsed in time with the vibrator, bound cock rubbing against the roughly carpeted floor of their play room. He had to be utterly desperate for more stimulation but Raina had no intention of giving it to him this soon.

"Be quiet," Raina said warningly as she pulled out of the kiss and backed away so that Tommy had nothing to touch, nothing to grasp.

She'd already forbidden him from touching himself. He could put his hands on the ground but not anywhere on his own body. Tommy swallowed down a desperate whimper that made her shiver at how delicious the boy was. Teolinda had been absolutely right that Tommy was a joy to play with. Instead of breaking her deliberately difficult to comply with rules, Tommy nodded and then placed his hands carefully on the floor in front of him.

His legs stayed spread wide, toes curling in arousal. Putting his hands on the ground made his back lengthen beautifully as well as lifting his butt so that she could see the vibrator pulsing away inside of him. Tommy shivered constantly but he managed not to do more than pant and whimper occasionally.

"Good," Raina crooned as she picked up her riding crop, looping the strap around her wrist. "Very good. Lift your ass."

Tommy went up on all fours so that his bound cock swung under his belly. It was nicely purple from the binding she'd tied around it. He was going to scream so beautifully when she let his cock free. His balls were hanging even further, tugged downwards by the weight she'd attached to the binding there.

But it was the vibrator that captured her attention. It jumped inside his ass, jerking rhythmically as Tommy repeatedly clamped down on it. Raina let out a long slow breath as her arousal shot up. Oh yes, Teolinda had definitely been right about Tommy's potential. If Felice weren't such a bitch about keeping her debt slaves Raina would have offered to buy Tommy off her.

"You look good this way," Raina murmured as she brought her riding crop down on Tommy's left butt cheek.

He jerked and gasped at the impact, head coming up sharply only to fall as he bit his lip to keep in another moan. The next blow two inches to the right made him buck and sway as if his arms weren't going to support him for much longer.

Raina grinned and kept hitting him with the crop. Spreading the blows out appeared to let him cope with the stimulation enough that he didn't collapse in a heap but when Raina hit the same spot twice, three times and then a fourth Tommy shouted and his arms dropped out from under him.

"Up," Raina said warningly as she raised the speed of the vibrator.

"Uhn!" Tommy grunted. "Uhn!"

He struggled to lift his face from the floor but his arms were shaking so badly that he couldn't keep himself up. Raina grinned as they collapsed out from under him again. His whimpers were a thing of beauty, especially as Raina drew her riding crop over the crack of his ass so that she could push the vibrator deeper into him.

A sharp shove made Tommy scream once, high and desperate and oh so sweet in his need. Raina growled as she went back to beating his ass. He would have bruises tomorrow, she decided. A vivid bruise on his left butt cheek that would make it impossible to sit down and a second bruise on the back of his right thigh exactly where it met his butt. She'd paid for the right to do whatever she wanted to his body short of scarring him so he'd take exactly what she gave him.

By the time the bruises were blooming on his pale, lovely skin Tommy's blindfold was visibly wet with tears. He didn't try to escape, didn't beg, didn't scream or break any of her other rules. Even more wonderfully he kept trying to get his arms back underneath him. Raina laughed with delight as he collapsed once more onto his face.

"You try so hard," Raina crooned as she bent to caress the blooming bruises. "You want to be good so very much. Don't you, Tommy?"

There was no proper way to respond to the question. If Tommy didn't respond then Raina could beat him. But if he did respond then she could punish him for breaking her order not to speak. Tommy shuddered and nodded as he struggled to lift his face back off the carpet again. The nod was so urgent, especially when coupled with his efforts to rise, that Raina almost felt bad about slapping the palm of her hand against Tommy's ass directly on top of the bruise.

Tommy shouted and collapsed again, making such a strangled noise that she knew he'd nearly come despite the bindings wrapped around his cock and balls. Raina laughed, delighted with his responses. It was almost worth pissing Felice off to get Tommy under her thumb but not quite. If he was female, yes, Raina would have contacted the DDSS with a bogus complaint in the off chance that she could buy him out from under Felice, even with the fines for false reporting.

"Such a good boy," Raina said as she turned the vibrator up to maximum. "Too bad for you that I'm not a good girl at all."

This time Tommy screamed. He screamed even harder as Raina stroked his bound cock and jerked on his balls just hard enough to make him really feel it. The added stimulation was finally enough to push Tommy over the edge into babbling pleas that made no sense, random words strung together that garbled on his tongue as he tried to crawl away from her on arms and legs that wouldn't cooperate.

Raina grinned as she grasped his balls, twisting on them so that he couldn't get away no matter how much he wanted to. It took one quick jerk at the bow knot securing the binding around his cock and balls to set them free. The thick leather strap slid loose easily, coming away in Raina's hand.

She tossed it aside as she leaned back to watch Tommy's reaction.

First he gasped at the release but the next second, as blood rushed back to his cock and balls, Tommy's whole body spasmed with pain. His babbling turned back into screams, perfect lovely screams, as he jerked and shuddered and then came from the combination of pain and pleasure. Better still, Tommy collapsed to the floor in an uncoordinated heap as he passed out.

Raina shuddered as she pushed him over onto his back so that she could straddle his limp body and rub off on his still ridged cock. She barked a shout as her orgasm thundered through her. Then she leaned on Tommy's chest as he groaned and started coming back to reality. His pained whimper at the pressure on his cock made Raina grin.

"Very good boy," Raina said. "I'm very pleased with you. What do you say, Tommy?"

"Thank you, Mistress," Tommy whispered, his voice so hoarse that she knew his throat had to be raw.

"Mmm, a very good boy indeed," Raina purred. "Now. I think I'll take off my clothes and you will stay right where you are. You're to suck on whatever I give you until I say to stop. Do you understand?"

"Yes, Mistress," Tommy replied.

His voice was a little stronger but he shook as if afraid of what she might do to him. Raina chuckled as she stood up to strip her clothes off. The hum of the vibrator was loud in the quiet of the play room. As she tossed her bra onto the bed Raina decided to leave the vibrator exactly where it was until it was time to leave. An ass that sweet needed to be filled.

∼

"Sit," Jerry sighed as the new boy, Tommy he thought, limped into Room B to debrief.

"No, thank you, sir," Tommy said.

His voice was so pained that Jerry raised an eyebrow and had the kid turn around. The livid bruises on his ass and thigh were so ugly that Jerry winced. He checked the agenda and nodded. Poor kind had gotten Mistress Raina, of all the bum luck assignments for him to get.

"Stand then," Jerry said as he turned the recorder on. "Raina Smith, served by Tommy Leigh. Speak slowly and clearly. Start with a recounting of events. Tell me everything that you learned that might be useful to Mistress Hong."

Tommy sighed at the standard spiel they all used to open the recording sessions. He leaned against the hard plastic chair, arms shaking and face pale enough that Jerry thought about sending him straight to the medics first. After a second Tommy shook his head and eased himself down into the chair. Sweat broke out on his forehead as he sat but apparently the cold plastic felt okay. There was only a little wince before the kid started talking.

"She said that Mistress Teolinda Horne had recommended me," Tommy began. "Apparently Mistress Teolinda has been recommending me to everyone."

"Ow," Jerry commented even though he should keep his mouth shut at this point in the interview.

"Yeah," Tommy said as he let out a breath that wasn't quite a sigh. "Anyway, most of what she talked about as she set up the rules and started the play was how annoying it was the Mistress Teolinda had cut her out of the McIntyre Munitions, Inc. contract. Apparently Mistress Raina's been working on getting the contract to produce the rocket shells for a couple of years. They lost the contract at the last second. Mistress Teolinda's company will be the one supplying the rocket shells which means that their plans to expand into military contracts have been blocked for the moment."

He shifted position and went so white that Jerry frowned at him. Tommy shook his head, hissing as he eased up off the chair and then settled back down carefully. The kid's expression was somewhere between agony and infuriated. Jerry didn't blame him. Those bruises looked seriously painful.

"I don't think they'll get the military contracts at all," Tommy said entirely too seriously for someone in that sort of pain. "I think that they've been blocked by far more than just Mistress Teolinda. From the way Mistress Raina acted and talked, her company's poorly run. She commented eight times on how much I looked like her 'fuck-up of a Production Manager'."

The air quotes plus Tommy's sardonic expression was enough to make Jerry grin. "Name on him?"

"She called him 'that fuck up Wentworth' or 'that asswad Louis' so I'd assume his name is Louis Wentworth," Tommy said. "I highly recommend checking him out. He might not actually be that bad at his job. Mistress Raina had an obvious fondness for setting up impossible situations and then punishing people for failing to deal with them. It was most of what we did tonight."

Jerry nodded. That matched what he'd heard from other debt slaves who'd served Mistress Raina as well as the profile he'd read before tonight's play began. That Tommy named Wentworth as worth of targeting meant that he'd need to spend a chunk of his free time after the interview researching what could be found out on the web. Wentworth might be ripe for turning and that was something that Mistress Hong always rewarded heavily.

"Another thing she mentioned several times," Tommy said with a tired sigh that spoke more of future pain than current, "is that her sisters are fighting her for control of the company. Their mother put it in the will that they're supposed to share the power. Mistress Raina complained about that several times, especially while she was fucking me. But apparently Paulin's trying to claim that Raina's too unpredictable and Idoberga's flying back from Sweden to contest both of their decisions at the big board meeting."

"Hell," Jerry swore as he noted that down and checked that his phone had enough power to call his supervisor. "When's that supposed to happen?"

"Two weeks," Tommy said so grimly that Jerry stared at him. "The board meeting is in two weeks unless Paulin manages to get it moved up. Even if she does, Idoberga's going to be in town in three days to fight them both."

Jerry stared at Tommy for a long moment, calculating how much trouble he'd get in for interrupting his supervisor at whatever he was doing versus getting Mistress Hong's organization moving quickly on Tommy's information. Tommy was in active pain, too. He should go see the medics about his bruises. But...

"Any internal damage?" Jerry asked.

"Not that I'm aware of," Tommy said so grimly that Jerry knew that the kid was figuring the angles just like he was. "No bleeding anyway. The bruises are nasty but that's not going to change much with ice packs or whatever."

"I'm getting my boss," Jerry said as he speed dialed and switched off the recording. "We need to get moving on this."

Instead of protesting the way Jerry half expected Tommy nodded, easing up out of the chair again for a moment before sitting in a slightly different position. Tommy hissed in pain but his smile got a little wider, a little colder and more calculating as he sat back down. He looked like someone who'd been a debt slave in the brothels for years, not less than a week. The hardness in his expression made Jerry wonder just how bad the service with Mistress Paulin had been.

"Do it please, sir," Tommy said.

The words were anything but a request. Jerry ignored the tone. If the kid actually had this good of information he was justified in making demands. Hell, if it was that good they might all get bonuses. Jerry could sure as hell use one. Unlike the prostitutes and spies, Jerry didn't get tips. This might give him the last bit he needed to get out of this hellhole and that was more than enough reason to sell Tommy's information hard once his boss picked up.

2. WAX

The wax hissed as it dripped down onto Tommy's cock. This candle was red and the pigments in it seemed to make the wax hotter if Tommy's gasp was anything to judge by. His body was a lovely patchwork of multicolored wax. Many of the blotches of wax cooled on top of bites that she'd give him after she'd gotten him tied up.

Tommy truly responded beautifully to such things. Teolinda had been quite right to praise the way he responded to bondage. Paulin's favorite leather cuffs kept him from moving even an inch especially with how tightly she'd stretched his arms and legs over the biggest bench. It was nicely padded, far more padded than Paulin liked for her playmates but that meant that she could keep him restrained for longer.

The smell of burning wax, leather and blood filled the room. Rather than use one of the opulent play rooms with their distracting scents and textures, Paulin had paid extra to use one of the bare rooms in the basement of the brothel. Most of the blood was from previous Masters' play with the whores who worked here. Some of it was Tommy's. Not much as she'd balked at paying the prices Hong wanted for scarring her prize new boy.

But a few bites that *accidentally* happened to break the skin here and there weren't the same thing at all. It was officially against the rules but so was beating Tommy's ass so hard that he couldn't sit down and Raina had done exactly that. Paulin wasn't all that worried about getting in trouble. She had enough money to pay both Hong's fees for 'undue damage' and to buy off the DDSS agent in charge of Tommy's case if necessary.

"I can see why you're worth so much money, Tommy," Paulin crooned as she poured more wax over his cock. "You do behave so very well."

"Th-thank you, Mistress," Tommy gasped, shuddering as the wax crept closer and closer to the tip of his cock. "Oh God!"

She grinned as she poured a long stream of wax directly onto the slit from less than an inch. Tommy jerked and panted, his eyes wide and mouth dropped open in pleasure mixed pain that he clearly had no idea how to deal with. Paulin watched his face avidly, soaking up the way he tried to gasp, tried to jerk, tried to make noises only to have them come out strangled and strange.

His responses were so perfect that Raina laughed as she used a butter knife to scrape the worst of the wax off his nipples, stomach and thighs. The red wax on his cock was too nice not to spread in other places. Tommy flinched and hissed as the knife ran over his nipples, his face going white in the bad ways instead of the good ones. Not that Paulin really minded hurting him in bad ways but she didn't want to do it accidentally. If she was going to do it she wanted to do it on purpose.

"What was that?" Paulin asked as she pinched one of his nipples.

"Eep!" Tommy gasped. "They're new piercings, Mistress."

"Newly pierced?" Paulin asked with much more interest than before. "You took the rings out for me, right?"

"Yes, Mistress," Tommy said, shaking at the look in her eyes. "Mostly healed but they're still a bit tender. Eep!"

This time when she pinched Paulin did it much more firmly. Tommy jerked hard against the cuffs, his breath stuttering and jerking as much as his body did. She grinned and pulled gently at first, then harder when he didn't scream so much as sigh very loudly. A sharp jerk got her the scream she wanted. Paulin laughed with delight before pressing a too-hard kiss against the nipple.

"Mmm, you really do have a lovely voice," Paulin murmured against his skin. The smell of wax and sweat filled her nose. She licked and chuckled at his whimper. "Oh, hush. I'm not going to do any serious damage to you, silly. I just like to get a real reaction."

"Mistress," Tommy said, his voice shaking in earnest, "please believe me. I've never done this before. Everything you're getting is real."

"I know!" Mistress Paulin laughed. "It's quite lovely. Now, I'm going to go back to covering your sexy little body with wax and then I'm going to let your arms free so that I can sit on your face for a while. It should be quite lovely. I do so love the smell and feel of wax on my partners."

His eyes went wide at the promise to let him eat her out. That was another thing that apparently Teolinda had been quite truthful about. Tommy looked like he'd let her do anything to him now, possibly including really hurting him, as long as he got to lick her pussy. Paulin chuckled as she took a new red candle and lit it from the last one.

"This will be so much fun," Paulin said as she poured the wax directly on a red spot on his thigh. Tommy gasped and jerked, making garbled noises that sounded like 'please' mixed with 'fuck'.

She really should lay off that spot if she wanted to avoid giving him burns but he responded so perfectly that Paulin laid down stripes and globs of wax over it instead. The other thigh wasn't quite as red but that was probably good. Paulin really shouldn't burn the boy. That would keep him from earning his living and the Good Lord knew that Hong charged her debt slaves for their food, water and lodging.

A nice puddle of wax in Tommy's bellybutton made a beautiful counterpoint to his pale skin. He cursed breathlessly as she did it but his cock never softened. When she moved up to cover his nipples again Tommy whimpered. The obvious begging didn't make it to his mouth so Paulin poured extra wax over his lovely nipples. With freshly pierced holes they had to be incredibly sensitive.

"Fuck, fuck, fuck," Tommy gasped. "Mistress!"

He jerked so hard against the restraints that the bench shifted slightly under him. Paulin laughed out loud and added a bit more wax and then more on top of that. By the time she was done covering his nipples with wax it looked as though he had pasties stuck on them. A bit more on top of that made it look like he was wearing a wax bra.

"Hmm," Paulin laughed. "I wonder if this is close to the bra you wore for Teolinda. Was it Tommy? Or was it a shelf bra? Maybe a push-up so that you could pretend to have cleavage? This looks more like a bikini than a real bra."

"Oh God, oh God, oh God," Tommy panted and shuddered, tears running down his cheeks. "Mistress, please, oh God, Mistress. It's too much!"

Paulin shuddered as hard as Tommy. She so loved it when she managed to break one of Hong's people enough to get them to beg. Rather than add more wax to Tommy's beautiful body, Paulin blew out the candle and then moved to let his arms go. She didn't let him immediately lower them. That would be cruel and besides it would disturb the wonderful patterns of wax she'd put on his body.

"Take it easy," Paulin crooned as she carefully helped Tommy lift his arm over his head and then slowly lower it down by his side. "You don't want to pass out just when we're getting to the good part."

"No, Mistress," Tommy said.

He hissed and shivered until both of his arms were safely resting on the bench by his sides. Paulin smirked as she secured them in place with a strap looped underneath the bench. She couldn't risk having him move and destroy the wax. That was her job, not his. Tommy didn't object to being restrained again immediately. In fact, he seemed to appreciate it.

"Now," Paulin said as she moved to straddle his head. "I want you to focus on making me come, Tommy. Teolinda said you were very good with that tongue of yours. So did Raina. I want you to show much just what you're capable of with nothing but your mouth."

"Oh God," Tommy moaned. "Please, Mistress!"

Before the words had been begging for Paulin to stop; this time they were a worshipful prayer for her to begin. Paulin shivered as she lowered herself onto Tommy's face, her fingernails already digging into the wax on Tommy's chest. Hopefully both Teolinda and Raina had been telling the truth about Tommy's oral skills. She loved being eaten out by an enthusiastic partner. If he did really well, Paulin would have to come back for more.

As soon as her clit was in reach Tommy latched onto it with his mouth, sucking so hard that Paulin gasped and jerked. The intensity shifted until Paulin started moaning and rocking against Tommy's mouth. Whatever he was doing with his tongue was brilliant enough that Paulin wasn't sure she was going to be able to hold herself up for terribly long.

"Oh fuck yeah," Paulin shouted. "Do that again!"

JERRY WAITED TENSELY for Tommy to come from his session with Mistress Paulin. Mistress Hong had been very pleased with his information the other night, so pleased that she'd deliberately invited both Paulin and her sister Idoberga to come and try out Tommy or another of the debt slaves with a discount. Paulin had accepted immediately, claiming Tommy. Jerry didn't know if Idoberga had chosen yet but she was due to come in tomorrow.

That would be exactly one week before the board meeting that everyone was working to find out about. Jerry hoped that Tommy had something useful when he got back to report. They needed something more than what they already had. His boss paced behind Jerry, cursing under his breath while chain smoking the most pungent, ridiculously vile cigars that Jerry had ever had to deal with.

"I need ice packs," Tommy said as he opened the door, before Jerry even realized that the door was opening. "Mistress Paulin left some burns with her wax play."

"How bad?" Jerry asked as his boss put out his cigar, thank fucking God.

He hissed as he saw the burns on Tommy's thigh, chest and stomach. Mistress Paulin should be paying some serious fees for damaging the goods, especially given that Tommy had a bite on his shoulder that was slowly seeping blood. It looked like it might have been covered in wax too. Flecks of wax covered his body from neck down to his knees with a big chunk clinging to his shaved testicles.

"On it," Bob, Jerry's boss, said. "Start talking, Tommy. Mistress Felice is hot on this one."

"Tell me about it." Tommy hissed as he sat down cautiously in the chair. "She was fierce when she gave me my instructions."

"Right," Jerry said as Bob hurried out to get the ice packs for Tommy. "Paulin Smith, served by Tommy Leigh. Speak slowly and clearly. Start with a recounting of events. Tell me everything that you learned that might be useful to Mistress Hong. What'd she say, kid?"

Tommy smiled at the way he rushed over the standard header, sighing with relief when Bob came back in with a medic, several ice packs and Mistress Hong herself. He didn't say anything until the medic had given him the ice packs and checked the bite on his shoulder. Wisely, Tommy only started talking once the medic was gone.

"The military contract they lost is only the tip of the iceberg," Tommy reported, talking straight to Mistress Hong rather than to Jerry, Bob or the recorder. "Mistress Paulin said outright that Idoberga suspects that either she or Mistress Raina is embezzling money from the company. Apparently their profits have been steadily falling for the last three years. It turned into a sharp drop since their mother died, though."

"Fuck," Mistress Hong cursed. "The company's falling apart?"

"Sounds like it, Mistress," Tommy said with a nod of confirmation that made him wince and touch the bite on his shoulder. "From what she said as she was cleaning herself up, Mistress Paulin isn't the one embezzling money. I don't actually think any of them are doing it. It sounded more like their policies have been messed up for so long that they've lost market share on all fronts. That plus their mother's death combined with the loss of the military contract hit their profits. It's bad business practices, not embezzling."

He sighed and shook his head at Mistress Hong's snarl. Jerry could understand why Mistress Hong was pissed. Pure bad business wasn't as useful for them as someone on the take. They'd do a lot better taking the Smith sisters down if they could turn them against each other. Tommy chuckled, his expression just wicked enough to make Jerry nervous. Both Bob and Mistress Hong didn't seem disturbed. They looked curious.

"The thing is," Tommy continued, "is that I don't think it matters that there's no one embezzling from the company. They're going to fight each other for control of the company. And then whichever of the sisters wins is going to tear the company apart looking for 'allies' that supported her sisters. The whole company is doomed. All it would take is a little push to set them at each other's throats."

"Now that's useful," Mistress Hong snapped. "Tommy, Idoberga is going to be in here in tomorrow. I'm going to push her straight at you. You have the most direct experience with Paulin and Raina. Do your best to make Idoberga believe that they think she's the crook. No..."

Mistress Hong stopped and grinned so evilly that all three of them shuddered. She rubbed her hands together before stabbing a finger in Tommy's face. He jerked and shivered, obviously terrified of Mistress Hong. Jerry thought he had every right to be. They all knew what happened to people who disappointed Mistress Hong. It had been too long since the last time Black came in to visit. Pissing Mistress Hong off right now was a guaranteed trip to the hospital care of Black's nonexistent mercies.

"Play the poor injured boy," Mistress Hong ordered. "Let her see the damage the other two have done to you. Play it all up, make it seem like you're traumatized and terrified.

Idoberga isn't the same sort of pervert as her sisters are. She'll be begging in your hands in no time, convinced that you're some sort of poor abused slave. Then push the idea that her sisters have to be embezzling from the company. By that point she should fall for it hook, line and sinker."

"Yes, Mistress," Tommy said.

3. BLOOD

"*I* truly have better things to do," Idoberga complained to Hong as they strode through the hallways of Hong's brothel. "My sisters are destroying the company and I only just got in from Sweden."

"Granted," Hong said with the sort of wicked smile that made Idoberga want to snap the little woman's neck. "But both of your sisters played with Tommy. Paulin talked about buying him from me, as if I'd sell, and Raina was... well. Severe. They both were. I need a third party besides the damned DDSS agent to verify what was done to him."

"They were that harsh?" Idoberga snarled, infuriated that her sisters were letting their more sadistic tendencies out in places where it could be discovered. "To a debt slave? Mother made it perfectly clear that they were never to do that!"

Hong shrugged. She didn't really need to say anything else. Mother was gone, leaving Idoberga, Paulin and Raina to run her company. Both of her sisters were clearly out of control. No matter how ridiculously obvious Hong's spying was, there was no reason to damage the debt slaves in her employ.

The darkly rich hallways gave way to a Spartan back hall that looked as though it had recently been painted. A few scuffs marked the walls in places but not many. Idoberga would have had words with Hong's cleaning staff. The stairs down to the basement where the debt slaves were kept while not working was terribly grubby, dirt piled in the corners though the treads were at least swept clean.

"He's in the infirmary currently," Hong said as she led the way down the long, obviously old and stained carpet that covered the hallway floor. "Burns, bites and some nasty bruises. His wrists are a mess. Between the two of them they managed to put a brand new boy completely out of commission for at least several weeks."

Idoberga growled. She wished her sisters were there right now. If Mother were still alive they would both be beaten to within an inch of their lives for crossing the line so badly. Truly, if Idoberga had a chance she would deliver the beating herself. Bad enough that they were embezzling money; damaging other people's employees so severely could not be tolerated.

The infirmary was small, clearly designed for treatment of minor injuries rather than anything more serious. Tommy, the boy her sisters had abused, was in a curtained off bed at the far side of the bright little room. Two other debt slaves were there, one with cane marks on his back and the other with an embarrassingly bright smile despite the cuts littering his body. Both of those debt slaves looked as though they were well used to rough trade and comfortable with what had happened to them.

"Tommy," Hong said in entirely too stern a voice for a traumatized debt slave, "we're coming in."

There was no reply but Hong didn't appear to expect one. She swept the curtain aside, gesturing for Idoberga to follow her. Tommy flinched when they entered the curtain, staring up at Hong and Idoberga with wide brown eyes filled with terror. Even though he didn't say a word, Idoberga could see him begging for them not to hurt him.

His shoulder had a bandage stained with blood that clearly came from a bite. Idoberga had seen enough similar bandages to know that Paulin was responsible for that. The boy also had salve-covered burns on his stomach, shoulder and one exposed thigh. He fidgeted at her stare, eyes snapping down towards his tightly clenched hands.

"Tommy, this is Idoberga Smith," Hong said. "She's come to verify your injuries."

"Yes, Mistress," Tommy said, his voice so rough that Idoberga was certain that he'd screamed his throat raw for one or both of her sisters. "Thank you, Mistress."

She could see him shaking just for her standing there looking at him. Idoberga bit down on the urge to swear in all the languages she knew. This could not be allowed to go unpunished. Her sisters had crossed the line one too many times. It would be dealt with severely this time so that it wouldn't ever happen again.

"Mistress Hong?" one of the medics called so hesitantly that Idoberga frowned. "Um, we have a situation with Urith."

"Fuck, not again," Hong groaned. "Tommy, I'll be right back. Damn it, what did those three morons do to him? He better not need to go to the hospital again!"

Hong strode away, closing the curtain behind her with a jerk that made Tommy flinch. His eyes were wide and frightened again but this time he was staring towards the curtain, not towards Idoberga. She frowned and touched just above the ligature marks marring his wrists.

"What's wrong?" Idoberga asked.

"Urith... was my roommate," Tommy whispered as more of Hong's furious cursing and worried shouts filled the room. "He, he does a lot of really rough trade. I. He's almost paid off his debt."

Idoberga frowned as she opened the curtain enough to check on this Urith. She winced at the amount of blood. The older debt slave lay limp on a stretcher, blood dripping down his arms and legs. It looked as though the trickle of blood was slowing and the man's skin was slowly turning grayish pale.

"Get a fucking ambulance now!" Hong bellowed. "Don't let those assholes leave!"

"Oh God," Tommy moaned.

He curled in on himself, exposing a terrible bruise nearly the size of his head on the back of his thigh. Idoberga sat on the edge of the bed and hugged the boy, holding him close as the medics shouted back and forth about IV's, blood transfusions and stabilizing Urith's heartbeat. They left the infirmary at a run, the wheels of Urith's stretcher rattling.

Tommy shivered nonstop in Idoberga's arms. When she looked through the gap she saw that they were alone. The other two debt slaves had been sent elsewhere and the medics had gone with Urith. Hong had apparently gone to deal with the vicious bastards who had nearly (actually?) killed Urith. Idoberga stroked Tommy's back as a thoroughly inappropriate thought occurred to her.

Tommy had been with both of her sisters. He spoke to them, listened to them. They had always been terrible about keeping secrets after they tortured someone. He might know which of them was embezzling funds from the company. Almost certainly he had to have heard bragging about what they wanted to do to her.

"Tommy," Idoberga said gently and quietly, hopeful that no one would hear her. They had very little time before Hong returned or one of her people came to guide Idoberga back to Hong's office.

"I, I'm sorry, Mistress," Tommy gasped, trying to pull away as if terrified that she'd beat him just for taking a hug that he so obviously needed.

"Shh, I am not upset, Tommy," Idoberga crooned as she pulled him closer and nuzzled the boy's lush brown hair. "I only had a question."

"I'm... I'm really not supposed to talk to customers without a play contract, Mistress," Tommy said. He twitched as if thinking about pulling away but another kiss to his hair made him sigh and relax in her arms. "Not supposed to."

"Mmm, I'm sure you're not, sweet boy," Idoberga said. She smiled sadly. He was exactly the sort of boy her sisters preferred to break. "I just wondered if my sisters spoke of me."

He flinched and sighed, nodding as he tucked his face into the crook of Idoberga's neck. It was a tender little move, or it would have been if Tommy hadn't started shaking so hard. She brushed her lips over his hair once more, rocking the boy very, very slightly. The little movement worked wonderfully to calm him. Idoberga couldn't help but wonder exactly how much affection Tommy got on a regular basis. He responded so strongly to it that she suspected he'd been abused long before he became a debt slave.

"They think you're embezzling money," Tommy whispered, shivering convulsively. "Both, both of them blame you. But..."

"But?" Idoberga asked, gently caressing Tommy's unbruised and unburned shoulder.

Tommy gulped, peering over her shoulder in fear of someone overhearing them. He buried his face against her neck and clung to her as if he was much younger than he appeared. Idoberga crooned again, rocking the boy until his shivers died down somewhat.

"But?"

"They both talked about... about their 'funds,'" Tommy whispered against Idoberga's neck. "Not, not like money they needed but... like funds set aside secretly. Something to give them more to work with."

Idoberga hissed, instantly infuriated. Of course they would. They couldn't consider their private little 'funds' to be embezzlement. Oh, no, only Idoberga could be doing that even though she had done no such thing. She carefully pushed Tommy away, holding his arms so that he had to meet her eyes. Tommy gulped and bit his lip but he didn't look away despite the fear making his eyes go wide.

"What do they intend to do?" Idoberga asked. She gave Tommy a little shake. "Little one, Hong will not be able to protect you from them. If I do not win against them they will come back and they will do damage beyond what you can endure. I would not have you end up like your friend Urith."

Tommy drew in a breath as he went so white that she feared he would pass out. He shook his head 'no' sharply, a bead of blood appearing underneath the teeth still clamped onto his lip. Idoberga cupped his face, rubbing her thumbs across Tommy's cheekbones. It made him still and stare. She could see his pulse begin to fall at his temples.

"Please, Tommy," Idoberga whispered. "Help me stop them."

"They didn't say much," Tommy whispered back, his lip clearly split. He didn't appear to notice the blood on his chin so she didn't draw attention to it. "Raina called you stupid, Mistress. She said that she had plans to destroy everything you cared about back in Sweden. I think... I think she meant your private companies but I don't know. It wasn't clear."

"That bitch," Idoberga huffed before shaking her head sharply. "I am sorry, Tommy. Was there anything else?"

"Raina kept saying that she had legal proof," Tommy said just a bit louder though still not loudly enough to be overheard. "I don't know of what. That's all she said: legal proof. She was... She's not a good person, is she, Mistress?"

"No, she is not," Idoberga sighed. "Neither of my sisters are good people."

Idoberga heard voices coming up the hallway, Hong's harshly shrill voice snapping orders to someone else. Their stolen private time was almost done. She smiled as gently as she could given how angry she was, pressing a gentle kiss against Tommy's forehead. He blushed brilliantly, covering his groin with both of his hands.

"Such a good boy," Idoberga crooned. "You behave, now."

"Yes, Mistress," Tommy said. His eyes drifted down to Idoberga's shirt, going wide with almost comic horror. "Oh no, Mistress! I stained your shirt!"

As Hong strode back in, her secretary right behind her with a tablet and a harried expression, Idoberga laughed. She patted Tommy's cheek fondly, ignoring the way he flinched from the slight impact. Yes, the boy had definitely been abused prior to becoming Hong's debt slave. Hopefully he would survive his time here better than his friend Urith had.

"Do not worry about it, Tommy," Idoberga said. "You worry about getting better. I have many shirts. Hong, I have seen enough. I will sign whatever statements you wish for the DDSS."

"Thank you," Hong said with an annoyed sigh. "I don't suppose you'd do so for Urith, as well?"

"Will he survive?" Idoberga asked as she moved to sign the tablet that Hong's secretary offered.

"They were resuscitating him on the way to the hospital," Hong growled, her fury obvious. "I don't know yet if he'll pull through."

"Then yes," Idoberga declared. "I will. Be good, Tommy. I will not allow my sisters to return here."

"Thank you, Mistress," Tommy said, the words a prayer of thanksgiving as well as simple gratitude.

Idoberga strode out of the infirmary with Hong by her side. Her mind was not on Tommy or Hong's many problems with the patrons of her brothel. None of that mattered. What mattered was keeping her sisters from destroying their company and from shaming the family with the base carnal desires. No matter what it took, Idoberga would stop them now that she knew what they were up to.

"So?" Jerry asked as Tommy walked in with Mistress Hong by his side.

"It worked beautifully," Mistress Hong gloated. "Good job, Tommy. Idoberga gave you a tip, by the way. Quite a nice one. Do a standard report. I want to know exactly what happened while we were faking Urith's death."

"Yes, Mistress," Tommy said.

He slumped into the hard plastic chair opposite Jerry as Mistress Hong strode out of the room. The door closed on her shouts to pick up the damn carpet and get things back to normal. Tommy rubbed the thread of blood on his chin off, his eyes dark and cynical as well as sad.

"It was really convincing," Tommy commented. "Urith. I thought he really was dying."

"You never know," Jerry murmured, his finger resting on the button for the recorder. "She... Mistress Hong likes her deceptions to be convincing to the authorities, Tommy. Urith might not actually make it."

As Tommy's face went white, Jerry pushed the button on the recorder, staring at its slowly ticking numbers rather than Tommy's horror. He really hated breaking the new kids in but what had to be had to be. Tommy moaned as Jerry cleared his throat.

"Idoberga Smith, served by Tommy Leigh. Speak slowly and clearly. Start with a recounting of events. Tell me everything that you learned that might be useful to Mistress Hong."

The End

AUTHOR'S NOTE: FEAST OF THE SENSES

The final story in this collection just had to be a happy one. For all the bad things that happen there are still couples who find each other. They make lives together, grow older and continue loving one another. We don't get many stories about happily married couples so I decided to share one in this story.

1. SOUND

"No peeking!"

"I'm not peeking," Wendell said with an aggravated sigh that echoed in Hilma's sparse dressing room. "I'm impatient. That's different."

Wendell listened as Hilma opened the closet, hangers rattling against the rod. Fabric rustled as she flipped through the various outfits Hilma so loved to collect. He could pick out the differences between wool and taffeta, silk and cotton. Hilma had insisted on this little exercise in cross dressing even though the party was about to start outside.

They'd already rolled silk stockings up Wendell's legs, securing them to smooth garters that fell from the bottom edge of a tight waist nipper. That had been a shock. Wendell had never worn one before. His waist was lean enough that it hadn't been necessary until tonight. He fidgeted, desperately wishing he could open his eyes but he'd promised to keep them shut until Hilma was done.

He jumped, gasping, as Hilma touched his shoulder. Something cool and slippery slid along his left thigh. The dress; it was the dress that Hilma wanted him to wear tonight. Wendell let out a long shuddery sigh. It was only the dress.

"Sure you are," Hilma said, amusement dripping from her voice as she manipulated the silk dress she as she wrapped it around Wendell's body, prompting him to lift arms and legs as needed. "You're nervous is what you are."

"I am not," Wendell protested automatically. Hilma always found ways to make him feel twitchy and nervous even when she was helping. "I'm... concerned. Gerard has never mentioned liking cross dressing, Hilma. He might not like this."

Hilma's laugh was more a loud, obnoxious snort of amusement. The chuckle that followed was just as bad, full of her snickering at his worries. Wendell didn't turn to glare over his shoulder at her. He wanted to but Hilma's temper scared him just enough that he didn't risk it.

Even though she was in a committed relationship with Jozef, Hilma always felt like a Dom to him. She was bossy, argumentative and domineering. But she was also incredibly good with fashion and oddly caring, especially for people she liked. Wendell wasn't sure what he'd done to earn her affection but she certainly seemed to approve of him. Sometimes he even thought that she liked him apart from his relationship with Gerard though he had no idea why.

"Darling, you're going to be fabulous," Hilma reassured him as she slid the zipper up with a tiny ratcheting growl, closing the dress around him. "The dress is perfect for your figure, especially with that waist nipper. Your make up is exquisite. You'll stun everyone with how good you look."

"But..."

Hilma gave his dress a couple of final tugs before resting her chin on Wendell's shoulder, hands warm and confident on his hips. She chuckled close to his ear, setting off shivers of involuntary arousal. Hilma pulled him around so that he could see his reflection in the mirror.

"Open your eyes, Wendell," Hilma drawled, low, amused, affectionate.

Ebony silk cascaded from his shoulders to his elbows in dramatic swags. The bodice skimmed his chest, tucked tight at the waist and then flared out into a wide froth of fabric that gave the illusion that Wendell was anything but male. Combined with the dramatic make up that Hilma had applied, Wendell could almost believe that he'd been transformed into a woman for the night.

"This..."

He waved his hands at the outfit, breath catching at the slithery sound of the silk moving around his body. Wendell had never worn anything this luxurious before. It looked incredible, felt even better, but he was almost afraid to breathe for fear of damaging the gorgeous dress.

"You're gorgeous," Hilma said, her smirk firmly in place as he stared at her. "And I know something you don't."

"What?" Wendell asked as his heart started beating faster.

That smile on Hilma's face always promised the most incredibly fun nights. She leaned so close that he could feel her breath against his chin. Her dangling earrings chimed like tiny bells as she chuckled once more. Hilma pursed her lips and then grinned at him.

"Gerard chose that dress for you."

This time her laughter made Wendell blush as he hurried as gracefully as he could to the drawing room where Gerard waited for him.

2. SIGHT

Hilma smiled as Gerard and Wendell danced together. The dress that Gerard had chosen was absolutely perfect for Wendell. The dark silk flowed perfectly around Wendell's athletic body, conforming and then releasing to give tantalizing glimpses of his physique. Better still, the color was perfect for him, highlighting his rosy complexion and fiery hair.

In contrast, Gerard had chosen a silver tuxedo that made him look as though he'd been carved from ebony. The man truly couldn't be more tempting if he tried. His power matched so very well with Wendell's grace. All around her Hilma heard people speculating about the two of them, crafting stories from their ignorance that ranged from visiting royalty from Europe to an African prince and his prized catamite on a night out incognito.

It made Hilma want to laugh, not that she would in such a public place. Jozef would be upset with her if she ruined his reputation by cackling like a goose at some of the ridiculous stories she overheard. The simpler truth didn't appear to occur to any of the fools surround Hilma.

This wasn't something grand or special. It was simply a night of pleasure for two people in love. Of course, in Hilma's opinion there was nothing more important in the world so she was glad that she'd had a hand to play in making the night happen for her friends.

"Ready to get something to eat?" Jozef murmured in Hilma's ear.

"Goodness, you startled me," Hilma said, hand pressed against her breastbone in a dramatic gesture that made Jozef smile like a shark.

Across the ballroom, Gerard pulled Wendell into a kiss that was just the right side of obscene. She smirked at the two of them. They wouldn't be in the ballroom very much longer. It was a pity that all her hard work was going to be tossed aside soon but that was all right.

She'd created the set dressing for their special night, nothing more. It was right and proper that it be abandoned when Gerard and Wendell headed upstairs to the play rooms. Jozef's hand tightened on Hilma's hip, promising similar fun for the two of them. Hilma looked over her shoulder at Jozef, her smile widening into something rapacious at the heat in his eyes.

"I suppose I could do with a nibble," Hilma murmured. A deliberate bat of her eyes turned the heat into amusement.

"Good," Jozef chuckled. "Come. I have something special set up just for you."

"Darling, you always know how to make my nights special," Hilma said as she looped her hand through his elbow. "Do lead on."

3. TASTE

Jozef licked the taste of strawberries from Hilma's stomach, smiling as she gasped and quivered. He could taste her sweat, the salt adding a perfect counterpoint to the sweetness of the berries. Outside people would still be dancing and talking, drinking bubbling champagne while discussing the latest movie or play, the smartest book or trashiest novel.

He couldn't care less about them. Hilma and her delectable body were all that mattered to Jozef. Kissing his way up Hilma's stomach towards her breasts gave him the taste of ham, then cheddar, then the whipped cream that he'd used to outline her breasts. Underneath him Hilma shivered and trembled at the effort of keeping herself still.

"I could eat them out of you," Jozef offered as he licked the chocolate sauce pooled at the notch of Hilma's throat. "I imagine three bananas at once is a bit much. They must be rather cold inside of you. Pity I couldn't have them warmed up prior to our... excursion into the pantry."

"You are an absolute bastard," Hilma gasped, her voice shaking with arousal. "Must I beg?"

"Mmm, yes," Jozef purred, leaning up enough that he could stare down into Hilma's eyes. "I think you must."

She bucked against his hips, sticky and desperate, panting so hard that he would have thought that she'd run a marathon rather than stay still while Jozef consumed his evening snack off her body. Hilma licked her lips, eyes half shut. The color on her cheeks was raspberry bold and twice as sweet as the best honey to Jozef.

"Please Master!" Hilma finally begged, giving him the title that she so rarely granted. "Please eat me!"

"Gladly my dear," Jozef murmured before capturing her lips for a quick brutal kiss. "They should be perfectly seasoned by now."

Hilma shouted as she came just from the thought of it. He laughed and moved down between her legs. Let others play with silk and whips. Jozef would always prefer the simpler pleasures of life. With three bananas to consume, a tray of condiments to sample yet and hours yet to go on the party he was certain he could keep them busy for quite some time to come.

4. TOUCH

$\mathcal{W}$endell's nails dragged over Gerard's back. He shivered at the pleasure-pain, feeling welts forming after Wendell's fingers had moved on to gouge into his ass. This had started out as a massage, another of Wendell's usually unsuccessful efforts to get Gerard to relax enough that his back didn't ache.

The play room was mostly empty, the other bunks around them unoccupied. Gerard could hear the sounds of pleasure coming from the other rooms but it was distant and unimportant compared to the feeling of Wendell's nails dragging over his skin, his breath gusting over Gerard's spine. Wendell had chosen one of the massage oils that heated when blown on. Every place his lips brushed against flared with tingling warmth that made Gerard shudder.

Breath ghosted over the small of Gerard's back followed by the flick of Wendell's tongue. Gerard jerked, a moan escaping his lips despite his intention to stay quiet through Wendell's massage. Most of the time Gerard ended up cursing Wendell out for the aches he woke. This time Gerard had promised to let Wendell do as he would.

"Shhh," Wendell whispered, his lips sliding up to nuzzle one of the welts on his shoulder blade. "Let me."

"Just... don't stop," Gerard said in a voice that came out far rougher than he'd expected.

Wendell laughed. His teeth bit down on one welt that felt as though it had bled. Gerard gasped and bucked involuntarily. As often as he'd bitten Wendell, Gerard had only rarely allowed Wendell to do the same. As arousal and need made Gerard's head swim he had to wonder why he'd been holding back.

"More?" Wendell asked in a rough whisper that made the hair stand up on the back of Gerard's neck.

"More!" Gerard barked. "Now!"

5. SCENT

"That was a good night," Wendell sighed, his pale face smiling in the darkness as if it was a beacon of everything good and right.

"Very," Gerard agreed.

He pulled Wendell closer so that they could wrap their arms around each other, breathing in the scent of Wendell's sweat mixed with the semen they'd both spilled. The party had gone long into the night, into the wee hours of the morning. Rose and gold tinted sunlight peeped through the blinds to slowly illuminate the play room. They'd ended up in one of the smallest play rooms, the one with bunks rather than large beds, mostly because everything else was full by the time they left the dance floor.

"You're still here," Jozef commented as he led Hilma through the play room towards the main stairway. "I thought the two of you went home hours ago."

"Oh no," Wendell laughed, smiling so brightly at Hilma that she laughed her brittle, authoritative laugh despite being naked other than a towel draped around her hips. "We got upstairs late and then never quite got around to seeing what everyone else was doing."

"The others are all gone," Jozef said. "Care to join us for an early breakfast?"

Wendell looked at Gerard hopefully enough that Gerard nodded yes. Getting up was a bit of a struggle that required both Wendell and Jozef's help. His back didn't appreciate all the dancing they'd done coupled with a night of highly enthusiastic sex on a less than supportive bed. But once vertical Gerard was perfectly mobile, thank goodness.

They left the sex-scented play rooms, Wendell and Hilma chattering about showers and massages, ruined pedicures and how many love bites they'd gotten. Jozef appeared to be content to let them rattle on about whatever they wished. Gerard was pleasantly exhausted so he had no interest in telling Hilma that she was a chattering goose to fuss over a pedicure when she looked that good at her age. The fight that would inevitably follow such a comment was far beyond his energy levels.

"Coffee," Gerard murmured to Jozef.

"Beverage of the Gods," Jozef agreed. "Especially when properly amended."

Jozef grinned at Gerard's raised eyebrow. He didn't explain what amendments he normally added to his coffee. Instead he lead them towards the scent of French Toast and frying bacon, one hand capturing Hilma's elbow when she started to go towards the private quarters of the mansion rather than towards the kitchen.

"Darling, I'm a disaster," Hilma protested, her free hand going to her hair.

"You're stunning," Gerard said. He grinned at Jozef's fierce look. "She is. Not the sort of stunning I find interesting in bed but stunning nonetheless. Your hair's fine, Hilma. Silver's a beautiful look on you. I'm glad you stopped dying it."

Hilma's smile was so brilliant that it all but glittered at him. Wendell laughed quietly, claiming Gerard's hand with a shy smile. They entered the kitchen that way, half dressed, obviously sex-drunk and sleep-deprived.

The huge kitchen was empty and quiet other than Jozef's chef. He smiled and nodded to them all, apparently quite used to having Jozef show up this way mornings after big parties. A pot of coffee already sat on the kitchen table, surrounded by a dozen or so mugs. Over a dozen tiny bottles of cream and flavorings sat with the pot of coffee, prompting Gerard to chuckle. So that was what Jozef had meant by amendments.

"Breakfast will be ready in ten minutes, Sir," Jozef's cook said. His accent was thickly Scottish despite the swarthy tone of his skin.

"Good, good," Jozef said. "I think we're all ready for some food."

"Very," Wendell said.

He pulled mugs from the collection while Hilma gracefully filled each one, leaving any addition of sugar or creamers to them. Jozef immediately began adding a few drops of each and every creamer to his mug while Hilma kept her coffee black. Gerard sipped his, sighing as the rich dark taste of truly expensive coffee filled his nose and mouth. He settled back into his chair, wincing briefly for the chill of the wood, slowly savoring his mug.

"Oh, what's that one?" Wendell asked. "Wintergreen?"

"It's glorious," Jozef said happily as he added three precise drops to his mug.

"I might have to try that but isn't it overpowering?" Wendell asked.

Gerard chuckled into his mug, meeting Hilma's eyes. The night had been something so close to perfection that Gerard almost wished that he could have recorded every precious moment. Between Hilma's help with the dress, the dancing and sex that followed, Gerard felt at one with the universe.

He breathed deeply, letting the bitter-sweet smell of the coffee fill his nose. A second breath gave him the scent of bacon, strawberries and cream, then butter sizzling in the pan. Gerard's lips curled against the rim of his mug as Wendell and Jozef's voices mixed with the smells and sensations to form a perfect moment in time, a snapshot of contentment that Gerard tucked away into the back of his mind.

"Don't add too much to it," Gerard commented as Jozef offered two more mint-based creamers to Wendell. "It's nearly perfect exactly as it is."

Wendell grinned, bright eyes sparkling with the same deep happiness that Gerard felt. The same happiness showed in Hilma's smirk and Jozef's triumphant smile as he stirred his thoroughly adulterated coffee. Gerard leaned over to press a kiss against Wendell's lips.

"What was that for?" Wendell asked, his forehead leaning against Gerard's.

"For you," Gerard replied as he rubbed his nose against Wendell's. "Just... for you."

THE END

OTHER BOOKS BY MEYARI MCFARLAND:

A New Path

Following the Trail

Crafting Home

Finding a Way

Go Between

Like Arrows of Fate

Out of Disaster

The Shores of Twilight Bay

Coming Together

Following the Beacon

The Solace of Her Clan

You can find these and many other books at www. MDR_Publishing.com. Sign up for our newsletter there and get updates on the latest releases plus a free book!

AUTHOR'S NOTE: THE NATURE OF BEASTS

Besides the previous collection of short stories in the Debts to Recover 'verse, there is one novel: The Nature of Beasts. It's a sweet story of recovering from abuse, not just for subs but also for Doms. I hope you enjoy the sample!

1. RETURNING HOME

Kaleb hummed as he carried the last box up the stairs to his new apartment. The hallway smelled of dust and the faintest traces of urine but Kaleb didn't care. In the next month or so the carpet would be ripped up and replaced, after the roof had been repaired. He was pretty sure that the windows would all have to be switched out as well. They were simple tempered glass with no laminated plastic or other security features if there was an attack in the area.

None of that was a surprise given how old the apartment building was. The stairwell up to the third floor showed the age of the building. Drab walls that had once been white were stained gray from time, punctuated by scuff marks and the occasional water stain under the window. It was an old building which suited Kaleb to the core. After all, he was an old man, or at least he felt like one.

The fire he'd felt in his twenties had long since burned down, leaving only embers behind. Part of that was the military contracts he'd worked on for the last fifteen years. Kaleb shuddered, one hand on the door knob as he tried to banish the memories of twisted bodies and burnt faces. Maybe he had made the world a safer place like General Reyes had shouted when Kaleb announced his retirement but Kaleb couldn't keep doing what he was doing.

"Mostly it's Todd," Kaleb whispered, a wry, exhausted smile twisting his lips. That mess had been what sent him into the military's arms nearly sixteen years ago. "Ah well, I still have a few boxes to unpack. No reason to keep wool-gathering."

After all the moving around he'd done in the last fifteen years, Kaleb had gotten used to living from boxes and keeping the absolute minimum belongs. It made for easy moving but he was looking forward to collecting things now that he was back in his home town. He'd already gotten his library out of storage. Having books around him was a joy that he'd found hard to live without.

"Have to call the contractor about getting the wiring checked," Kaleb muttered as he let himself into his apartment.

The light outside flickered randomly, apparently in response to the wind. Inside, the walls were freshly painted in a soothing creamy white. He'd had the carpet ripped up and wood floors put down before he moved in. The kitchen was tiny, barely big enough for one, much less two, but the appliances were relatively new. His whole apartment smelled new. It was something he looked forward to fixing once he was able to do some cooking. A nice spicy chili verde and some bread would do wonders for his apartment's scent.

Kaleb deposited his last box on the steel counter and smiled. Yeah, it was a good apartment, not the best in the city but also not in a terrible neighborhood. His neighbors on this floor looked to be reasonable, with a young family, an older man and then the mystery neighbor that he had yet to see during the two days he'd spent moving in. None of them seemed to be the type for loud parties or fighting, making them ideal as far as Kaleb was concerned.

He stretched and quietly cursed the fact that he was getting older for perhaps the millionth time. Five years ago he would have been able to carry all the boxes and still have energy to spare. Kaleb huffed a laugh, shaking his head at himself. His aching back would just have to be endured.

"I sound like my father," Kaleb said as he headed back down the three flights of stairs to his borrowed truck. "Well, not really. Father wouldn't have sold the company and gone to work for someone else but still. Now I know what he meant about the pain of getting older."

The drive across town highlighted the changes that had happened while Kaleb was gone. Not one tree stood on the streets. They'd all been cut down when Black started his terrorist campaign. Every window had bars. Most had steel shutters that would slam into place at the first sign of trouble. The cars that Kaleb passed were mostly armored and the big bus that carried the poor people around town looked like a tank, not a civilian vehicle.

Kaleb's car, left at his friend Jack's home during the move, was far more discreetly armored, as well as more effectively. Despite his certainty that his car could survive several direct rocket blasts, Kaleb hadn't wanted to risk that it would be stolen. Reclaiming his car was the work of minutes despite Jack's attempts to invite Kaleb in for dinner and romp with his long-time submissive debt slave Alice.

Of course, Kaleb refused politely. The offer had been more of an offer to let them share Alice than it was to share a meal. It was a long-standing one that Kaleb tried not to resent as he thanked Jack again before he left in his own car. They had stayed friends despite Kaleb's long absence and his inability to talk about the projects that he'd been working on for the military.

"Still don't need a slave," Kaleb grumbled as he waited at a stop light for a dozen or so heavily armored police trucks to barrel down the crossing street, sirens wailing and lights flashing. "And I don't like the idea of sharing Alice, sweet girl though she is. She deserves his undivided attention."

He drove onwards once the lights changed. One of the other drivers at the stoplight gave Kaleb an odd look. It was only then that he realized that he'd left the window open and that he was talking out loud. Kaleb rolled the window up again, chuckling at himself. Military bases were so much more secure that he'd gotten out of the habit of taking precautions all the time. The issue of talking to himself was never going to be solved; that was a facet of his personality that had been there since he was tiny.

"Home is such a nice word," Kaleb mused as he headed back into his apartment after locking his car in its secure garage in the basement. "About damned time I let myself have a home again."

For the first time, when he entered the hallway to his apartment the door that led to his mysterious neighbor's apartment was open a crack. Kaleb smiled at the thin sliver of young black man that he could see, jumping when his mystery neighbor slammed the door and threw the locks in quick succession. Kaleb raised an eyebrow at the severity of the response but it was hardly his place to be upset by another person's nervousness. For all he knew the boy was an agoraphobe who couldn't stand being around strange people.

The next week, spent unpacking boxes, rearranging his apartment and fielding calls from old friends delighted to hear that he was back in town, gave him more opportunities to wonder about his neighbor. Between trips down to the dumpster to get rid of empty boxes, Kaleb caught glimpses of the young man.

Approximately twenty years old, with sable brown skin, a shaved head and wide dark eyes that got wider whenever he interacted with Kaleb, his neighbor had the sort of skittishness that screamed abuse and stalking. His clothes were clean but threadbare and his shoes looked as though they were about to fall apart at any moment. Worse still, he was so thin that Kaleb was tempted to introduce himself just so that he could feed the boy.

It took three weeks before he actually held a conversation with his neighbor. Late one night, after cooking dinner and realizing that he had to take out the trash or the apartment would smell of salmon and spinach for days, Kaleb opened his door to find his neighbor almost directly in front of his face. His neighbor had several new bruises around his mouth and neck as well as a pathetically small bag of laundry in his arms.

"Sorry," Kaleb said with a polite nod and a wry smile. "Just running the trash. I can go first if that makes you more comfortable?"

"Uh, yeah," the young man said. "Please."

He swallowed so hard that the heavy leather collar around his neck bobbed. The lock holding his collar shut was so large that it had to be intended for use locking up buildings and the like. It certainly wasn't intended for wearing on a collar. Kaleb could see that it made the collar far more uncomfortable than it should be.

As soon as his neighbor noticed Kaleb's eyes on the lock he slapped a hand over it, looking away uncomfortably. Rather than make him any more uncomfortable, Kaleb nodded to his neighbor and headed downstairs with his garbage. He made a point of humming cheerfully despite his worries about the young man.

Something was clearly going very wrong with his neighbor's relationships if that was the condition he was in. The boy had that 'please don't hurt me' look that Kaleb had always associated with abuse victims prior to escaping from the cycle. His extreme avoidance was another sign of it. With those facts and the excessively heavy lock on his collar, Kaleb was fairly certain that he could get the police to intervene.

Not that it would do much good if his neighbor wasn't ready to escape. Kaleb just hoped that it wouldn't take a true medical disaster for his neighbor to realize that he deserved better. He'd seen the cycle of abuse eat so many people alive.

The dumpster was full, necessitating Kaleb to push other bags of garbage down so that his bag would fit. The smell was horrific but a good wash of his hands once he was back inside would take care of that. At least he wouldn't wake up to the smell of salmon in the middle of the night. He gently closed the lid of the dumpster and headed back inside, only to encounter his neighbor coming out with his laundry.

"Go right ahead," Kaleb said graciously as he held the door for his neighbor. "If you need anything don't hesitate to holler. I'm getting old but I do what I can for my neighbors."

"Thanks," his neighbor said, looking uncomfortable as he hurried down the stairs and then out of the alley towards the street like his ass was on fire.

"I wonder if I can find out who your Dom is," Kaleb murmured once his neighbor was out of sight. "There has to be some information about him and you."

The urge to interfere warred with Kaleb's bone deep tiredness with rescuing people only to have them walk away. He took extra time washing his hands, letting the soap suds mound up only to rinse them away under water that was a shade too hot. The sound of the water running into the sink, drumming on the steel basin, somehow summoned all the battles with Todd.

"I'm not your fucking pet! Stop treating me like I'm an animal that just needs some petting and discipline to behave better!"

"I'm not!" Kaleb had shouted back. *"I'm acting like a Dom who's had enough of his sub's arrogance and undeserved pride. I just asked you to do the laundry, Todd. I'm working a full day and you're home. It's a simple enough task."*

"You're rich enough to hire an army of servants," Todd had hissed at him, eyes wild with anger and fear and lust that made Kaleb's heart ache even after all these years. *"You don't need me to do things for you. You just want to watch me crawl for whatever scraps of affection I give you!"*

Kaleb shuddered as he blindly turned the water off. The fights had only gotten worse after that. He'd thought that he could get through to Todd, that he could show Todd that learning restraint and personal discipline in areas outside of the bedroom helped make one a better person and a better sub. But none of the lessons appeared to get through to Todd. Nothing Kaleb had done had gotten through to him, up to and including the day when Kaleb had come home, gotten in another fight and had enough.

Throwing Todd out had been the hardest thing that Kaleb had ever done. His white face and screams of enraged fear still haunted Kaleb's nightmares. Kaleb wiped off the counter, filled and started the dishwasher. He swept the floors, dusted the bookshelves, stripped the bed and then remade it despite having put new sheets on just two days before.

"I don't want another slave," Kaleb whispered once his house was as much in order as it could possibly be. He put his face in his hands and shuddered. "I don't want a sub. I don't want anyone. I don't."

Sleep was a long time coming that night. When it finally came Kaleb dreamed of his neighbor being beaten by Todd. In the dream Kaleb begged Todd to stop only to have Todd turn and smile at him, the same bright, cheerful smile that had marked the beginning of their relationship.

"But this is what you taught me to be," the dream Todd said.

"This is what I tried to save you from!" Kaleb cried, trying to wrench his neighbor away from Todd and failing because the two of them might as well have been made from marble. *"This is abuse, Todd. It's not love. It's not what he wants!"*

"How would you know?" Todd asked, still with that cheerful expression but now in the angry, resentful tone of voice he'd used at the end. *"Did you ask?"*

He woke in the middle of the night to stare at the ceiling for a very long time. Kaleb sighed. He hadn't asked his neighbor anything about his situation. It might be completely consensual but Kaleb doubted that. The fearful expression made Kaleb think that it might have started out consensual but it clearly wasn't anymore.

Three days passed before Kaleb had another chance to interact with his neighbor. He'd started working part time at a local bookstore more for something to do than out of any need for the money. His retirement money from the military was more than adequate and Kaleb still had all the profit he'd made when he sold the family businesses. Still, it was good to talk to people and do things outside of his home. The last thing Kaleb wanted was to become a hermit.

The day had been busy, full of people and unboxing a shipment of books. Kaleb had spent longer than normal there, reading as well as working. Then he'd gone out to dinner due to a complete lack of interest in cooking after the day he'd had.

All of that got him home well past his habitual bedtime. His bedroom was well soundproofed, something he'd insisted on before moving in, so Kaleb cursed under his breath as he ran up the stairs towards the sound of his neighbor begging and whimpering in pain. If he'd been more aware of what happened outside of his apartment maybe he could have prevented the assault from ever happening.

Because it was an assault. Kaleb emerged from the stairwell to see his neighbor pressed against the wall opposite Kaleb's door with his pants around his knees and his face smashed against the wall. The boy's cock was limp, the balls so tight against his body that Kaleb knew that this wasn't something he wanted. The man holding him there was bigger, stronger, dressed in the sort of cheap black leather that thugs wore when they tried to pretend that they were Masters.

Kaleb didn't remember charging up the hallway. He didn't quite remember kicking his neighbor's assailant in the back of his knees but having done that Kaleb didn't hesitate to grab the other man's head and smash it against the opposite wall.

"No!" Kaleb's neighbor wailed.

"I'm gonna kill you, you stupid bastard!" his assailant shouted.

Kaleb smashed his head against the wall again, hard enough to break the sheetrock and the man's nose. Blood splattered and dripped down the wall, flowing down the man's face when Kaleb pulled him back. He didn't bother to say anything in response to the man's shouts and cursing as he hauled the man down the stairs and out into the alley behind their apartment building.

"You're going to pay for this you stupid son of a bitch!" the would-be Dom shouted.

"Wrong," Kaleb snapped.

"Fucking--!"

The rest of what he'd been about to say was cut off as Kaleb jabbed the younger man in the gut, precisely hitting his solar plexus. Air whooshed out of his lungs as he doubled over. Kaleb kicked his right kneecap, dislocating it and causing a scream that had the rest of his neighbors opening curtains and staring down at them. The would-be Dom toppled to the ground, glaring at Kaleb as he tried to struggle back to his feet. Simply putting his hand around the man's neck and pressing against his windpipe was enough to keep him on this knees despite the pain of his dislocated knee.

"This is my home," Kaleb growled at him. "You will not indulge in this behavior here. I will not allow it."

"The fuck!" the creep growled, gasping as his attempts to break free and stand resulted in Kaleb compressing his windpipe to the point the man couldn't breathe while digging his nails in hard enough to break the skin on the back of his neck.

"I repeat," Kaleb said, dropping his voice into his long-abandoned Master's tone of voice, "you will not do this here. This is my home. You will leave. If you ever return I will show you exactly what I'm capable of before delivering you to the police."

Kaleb didn't expect that the threat would be effective. The would-be Dom's angry expression showed no signs that he understood that he was dealing with a true Master and a military-trained one at that. It was more or less inevitable that the creep would be back to terrorize his neighbor before too long though hopefully the dislocated kneecap would slow him down enough that he wouldn't be effective.

Not that Kaleb intended to give him the chance to come back. He let the would-be Dom go, jerking his chin towards the end of the alleyway. It took three tries before the man was able to stand but once he did, the would-be Dom snarled at Kaleb.

"You are so dead!" he snapped. "I have friends. They're going to make you wish you'd never been born."

"My friends run the city," Kaleb replied as he sent the would-be Dom back to the ground with a series of punches that broke his cheekbone, several ribs and possibly gave him a bone-deep bruise on his injured leg. "They run the military.

They run the police. Go or I'll give them your dead body to bury."

That threat seemed to get through to the would-be Dom or maybe it was the amount of pain he was in. This time when he struggled to his feet, he staggered towards the end of the alley, cursing Kaleb with every wobbly step he took. Kaleb sighed and shook his head. He would have to call the police about that one but first he needed to check on his neighbor and make sure that he was okay. That came first.

THE NATURE OF BEASTS is now available at all major retailers in ebook and TPB format.

AFTERWORD

Tommy is one of my favorite characters. I think that probably shows. He goes through a lot in these stories and starts growing up very rapidly. Unfortunately for Tommy there's a lot more growing up for him to do.

In this world, it's the people who can lock their hearts away while they do whatever they have to that get ahead. It wasn't always that way. Right now Tommy thinks that he can survive being Felice Hong's debt slave more or less intact.

Unfortunately for Tommy, that may not be true. Mistress Felice Hong's brothels are meat grinders. Beautiful, intelligent young people go into them. Not many come out intact. Quite a few, more than is reasonable, don't come out at all.

It's a fact of life that Tommy's still coming to accept. I hope that you enjoyed this story. Please consider checking out my other stories in this 'verse and thank you for reading!

Meyari McFarland
   September, 2013
   www.MDR-Publishing.com

AUTHOR BIO

Meyari McFarland has been telling stories since she was a small child. Her stories range from adventures appropriate to children to erotica but they always feature strong characters who do what they think is right no matter what gets in their way.

Meyari has been married for twenty years and has no children or pets. She lives in the Puget Sound, WA and enjoys the fog, rain and cool weather that are typical here. When vacation times come, she and her husband usually go somewhere warm like Hawaii or they go on their own adventures to Japan and other far away countries.

Her life has included jobs ranging from cleaning motel rooms, food service, receptionist, building and editing digital maps, auditing and document control.

More from Meyari McFarland

WEBSITE:

. . .

www.MDR-Publishing.com

Social Media:

Facebook - https://www.facebook.com/meyari.mcfarland.5
Instagram - https://www.instagram.com/meyarimcfarland/
Tumblr - https://www.tumblr.com/blog/me-ya-ri
Pinterest - https://www.pinterest.com/meyarim/

If you enjoyed this story, please leave a comment on your favorite site. Also, please sign up for the newsletter so that you can hear about the latest preorders and new releases.

www.ingramcontent.com/pod-product-compliance
Lightning Source LLC
LaVergne TN
LVHW041636060526
838200LV00040B/1595